BRAM STOKER'S
Dracula

BRAM STOKER'S

Dracula

The Novel of the Film Directed by
FRANCIS FORD COPPOLA
By FRED SABERHAGEN and
JAMES V. HART
Based on the Screenplay by
JAMES V. HART
From the Bram Stoker Novel

A SIGNET BOOK

SIGNET
Published by the Penguin Group
Penguin Books USA Inc., 375 Hudson Street,
New York, New York 10014, U.S.A.
Penguin Books Ltd, 27 Wrights Lane,
London W8 5TZ, England
Penguin Books Australia Ltd, Ringwood,
Victoria, Australia
Penguin Books Canada Ltd, 10 Alcorn Avenue,
Toronto, Ontario, Canada M4V 3B2
Penguin Books (N.Z.) Ltd, 182-190 Wairau Road,
Auckland 10, New Zealand

Penguin Books Ltd, Registered Offices:
Harmondsworth, Middlesex, England

First published by Signet, an imprint of New American Library, a division of
Penguin Books USA Inc.

Copyright © 1992 Columbia Pictures Industries, Inc.
ISBN: 0-451-17575-1
Photos: Ralph Nelson
All rights reserved

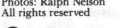 REGISTERED TRADEMARK—MARCA REGISTRADA

Printed in the United States of America

A NOTE FROM
THE SCREENWRITER

Dear Reader,

What follows here is not Bram Stoker's 1897 novel, which I urge you to read if you have never taken the opportunity, but Fred Saberhagen's retelling of the motion picture called *Bram Stoker's Dracula*. The book you hold in your hand is based on my screen adaptation of that classic story, which Francis Ford Coppola has directed with a masterful hand and eye.

How is this telling different from Stoker's original? Where the spirit of this novel is faithful to Stoker, it is also a departure. The question has been asked, "How did Dracula become a vampire?" In my research into the historical Dracula, aka Vlad the Impaler, I was surprised to learn that the true Dracula was a holy knight of the church, a member of the Order of the Dragon—a sacred order sworn to protect the church from all enemies of the cross of Christ. This man was a charismatic, heroic crusader who, in the 1400s, saved his Christian homeland from invasion by Moslem Turks. Somehow, this did not strike me as the popular, conventional wisdom of Dracula as a God-hating, crucifix-fearing, bloodsucking beast of the night. The man defended the cross—he didn't shrink from it.

Another discovery further revised my "conventional wisdom" of the Dracula myth. Prince Dracula's wife committed suicide when she was wrongly informed that Dracula had been killed by the Turks. Since she took her own life, her soul could not enter the gates of heaven; she was eternally damned by the laws of the very church her prince had defended with the blood of thousands he had impaled and tortured.

All the pieces suddenly fit for a retelling of Dracula which

5

combines the historical Dracula with the Dracula of Stoker's fiction. Here is a great warrior who loses his one true love and vows to return from his own grave to avenge her death. Dracula rises from death as a fallen angel at war with God, cursed to walk through the centuries, feeding on living blood, until he finds true love again four hundred years later, in late nineteenth-century London. Mina, Jonathan Harker's bride-to-be, is the true love Dracula has yearned for during his exile from the living.

This Dracula is the untold story of a true love that never dies.

JAMES V. HART
Los Angeles, 1992

PROLOGUE:
EASTERN EUROPE, 1462

Ever since her young prince had ridden away to war, the sleep of the Princess Elisabeth had been tormented by red dreams of horror and blood. Each night the princess fought as long as possible to stay awake; and when inevitably, sooner or later, she yielded to nature and closed her eyes, she soon found herself wandering amid nightmare fields of impaled bodies and amputated limbs. Again she fought as long as possible to keep from looking at any of the maimed soldiers' faces—and again, sooner or later, she was compelled to confront one of them.

The face of the mangled prisoner was always *his*, and always Elisabeth woke screaming.

Tonight, in the hour before dawn, the hour of her deepest despair, Elisabeth paced the rooms of her high apartment on the safest side of the castle, while her serving women, exhausted by the near madness of their mistress, slept. Now in the lady's waking imagination, even as in her dreams, the sanguine fluid ran thick and red from the veins of her young husband and lover; claret pressed from his body drop by drop, torn from him by the merciless instruments of the faceless Turkish torturers who held him as their prisoner.

Ceaselessly tonight the wind whined around the battlements and entered through her window open to the night, making a sound of dying groans, departing souls. The vision of the prince's suffering and death could neither be endured nor avoided. Useless to tell herself that all the fear and horror was baseless, that she had no certain knowledge that her husband was a prisoner of the Turks, no concrete evidence he had been captured, slain, or even injured.

7

But the only certain knowledge this lady had, assured her that the world was filled with death and terror, and that the only fate of a soldier's woman was to mourn.

In her present state of fear and exhaustion the lady was only half-aware of her immediate surroundings. She had interrupted her pacing in the one room of her apartment where there was light. Here, a dying fire smoldered on the small hearth, and the flame of one candle, burning on a central table, held back the predawn darkness that loomed outside the open window. Fireplace and candle together produced dim wavery illumination only suggesting the colors of tapestry and arras on the walls, and of the silken hangings of the curtained bed where *he* had claimed her as his bride.

In that bed he had held her against his heart, promised her he would return. There he, her noble prince, had bound her to him with such love that if he were dead—she knew it!—the light of her own life would go out like a small candle.

Even as the princess stood there in trembling contemplation, the arrow entered the apartment gently, fluttering through the high window as weary as a tired bird, flying at the very peak of the tallest curve of flight along which strong arms and a fine bow had been able to propel it. Before she had even recognized the nature of the messenger, the dark-haired lady recoiled from it, as she might have from some feathered flying demon, with the despairing shriek of one who knows that her own soul is lost.

The iron point of the war arrow, cruelly barbed, bit weakly at the soft wax of the lone candle, toppling candle and golden stick upon the solid wooden table. The single flame went out.

The Lady Elisabeth remained in the position of her horrified recoil, her face of classic beauty frozen like that of a statue, dark eyes staring at her doom. The dying fire upon the hearth, combined with the full moon setting outside the western window, gave light enough to show her that the messenger bearing her doom had come in the form of an arrow, wearing a small collar of white paper, tightly wrapped.

In a moment Elisabeth had embraced her demonic visitor and was opening the small wrap of fine white paper, gazing at the message that it bore. The Latin learned in girlhood came back to her—but even before she read the murderous words, she knew that they announced *his* death—and therefore hers.

It took her only a minute, moving now in the calm of utter madness and despair, to relight the candle, find more paper, and write the note that she must write.

A minute after that, running, climbing in a frenzy, she had reached the highest battlements, winning a race there with the first rays of the sun. The morning breeze, under the great dome of sky now painted with the dawn, blew at her raven hair. Far, far below, still wrapped in night, the river wound beneath the high-walled castle on its hill.

Screaming her lover's name, the Princess Elisabeth ran swiftly, eager to join him there below in darkness. The stones of the parapet came rushing beneath her feet. And then her feet were treading only air.

Many hours later on that same day the prince himself, with a portion of his army, returned to his castle from a successful defense of his homeland against the Turks.

The young warlord rode near the center of a thin column of tired, hard-bitten foot soldiers. The men were marching briskly despite all the miles and all the fighting they had put behind them in the last few months. They were covering the ground swiftly, at route step, because at last, having endured so much blood and terror, having suffered so many casualties, these men were coming home. They were leaving behind them the horror, the slaughter of the wounded on both sides, the fields of impaled prisoners' bodies.

The road—here, far from any major city, it was little more than an ascending track—came winding in from the east, and it carried the marchers, now squinting into the afternoon's declining sun, up into the high Carpathians. As always in spring, this country, their homeland, bloomed with a bewildering mass of fruit blossom— apple, plum, pear, and cherry. On both sides of the marching column lay a green, sloping land, full of forests and small woods, with here and there steep foothills crowned with clumps of trees or with farmhouses.

Most of the men in the long veteran column shouldered spears, some of them bore long swords or other weapons. Only a few were mounted; and most conspicuous among these was their com-

9

mander. He, the prince, was as battle-weary a soldier as any of them, but distinguished by his red armor, metal and cloth once bright and new, now battered and stained by war. A distinctive helmet was slung behind the leader's saddle, along with the javelin that complemented the sword belted at his waist. A shield, marked with the insignia of the Order of the Dragon, hung on one side.

This afternoon the months of yearning and doubt and danger were over at last, and he was almost home. He spurred his powerful black war-horse, urging the animal up a difficult, winding road, to where a distant castle had now come into view, gray and stark against the sky.

A quarter of a mile below the castle the warlord paused, his face softening. It was as if, for the first time in months, life and hope were now daring to flood back.

"Elisabeth," he murmured, as a man dying of thirst might have uttered the word *water*. The prince spurred his weary mount again, pressing forward past the thin file of his shuffling, almost exhausted foot soldiers, his countenance like theirs alive in the late-afternoon sunlight with the thoughts of rest and peace.

But before the warrior had covered half of the remaining distance to the castle, he reined in his stallion again. Unfamiliar black banners fringed the castle walls, a solemn funerary chanting of monks' voices came drifting downhill on the sunset breeze. And for a long moment, as sometimes happened in battle, it seemed to the returning soldier that perhaps his heart had stopped.

Yet once more he spurred his great horse, this time savagely. Thundering past an outer gateway, traversing a grim gloomy tunnel built through mossy stone, the commander, his face now pale, reined his war-horse to a halt in the middle of a large inner courtyard, where he leaped from the saddle.

Many people were gathered in the courtyard when he arrived—servants, relatives, neighbors, a few old friends, comrades-in-arms—but the returning lord of the castle had no time for any of them now.

Before the noise and dash of the prince's arrival, all of their attention had been focused on the dark doorway of the chapel, and on what was going on inside.

It was from that dark doorway that the mournful chanting sounded.

The tall, lean figure of the lord of the castle strode in through the dark doorway. Inside, a hundred or more candles burned, but most of them were set on and around the high altar at one end of the large chapel, so that their flames only seemed to intensify the gloom in the dim chamber's farther reaches. As many folk seemed to be crowded in here as had been standing in the outer court. But still the man who had just arrived had eyes for only one face, one figure. His whole attention was riveted on the slight, pale, lifeless form of a young woman.

Dark-haired, and with the beauty of her face still spared by death, she lay on a low flight of stairs at the far end of the chapel, beneath a great stone dragon arch, directly before the tall altar with its many candles and its great wooden cross.

Uttering a wordless, animal cry of fear and pain, the returning prince went stumbling, rushing forward. He halted, arms helplessly outspread, just before the body.

"Elisabeth!" This time the name seemed torn from him by some force that might equally have wrenched out his own soul.

The dead woman lying before him was still clad in rich garments that she must have worn in life; and her clothing most strangely dripped with water, so that the folds of fabric clung closely, wetly to the lifeless form beneath.

But it was not only water that saturated the clothing and stained the shallow steps on which the body lay, trickling down them to the stone floor. The corpse, horribly broken and battered under the concealing dress, still oozed blood.

In the awful silence following that terrible cry, the chief among the priests, distinguished from the others by the brightness of his ceremonial robe, moved a step forward.

The priest cleared his throat. Deferentially but firmly he began: "Prince Dracula—"

But the warrior was paying not the least attention. Instead he knelt, then crumpled forward, prostrate over the woman's body, groaning, kissing, and caressing the dead clay, futilely willing it back to life.

Long moments passed, during which the prince's shoulders gradually ceased to shudder with his sobs, and he became as still as the one he mourned.

Utter silence reigned in the chapel now; the chanting of the monks had ceased.

At last, slowly and painfully, the lord regained his feet. He swept his piercing, blue-eyed gaze across the semicircle of people standing just below the steps.

11

"How did she die?" His tone was deep and hollow.

The silence held. No one wanted to reply to that question. Perhaps none dared.

The prince's face began to alter, total grief making room for the first hint of a still-formless suspicion, presaging terrible anger. He focused on the monk who had addressed him earlier.

"How did she die, Chesare?"

The monk, tall and impressively robed as if for some important ceremony, once more cleared his throat.

"She . . . fell, sire. From the battlements onto the rocks . . . into the river."

"Fell? Fell? How is that possible? How could my wife have fallen?"

Again, only silence answered. No one had an explanation ready—or none dared to put one into words.

At last it fell to the priest, again, to find some way to speak the unhappy truth. "My son—the Princess Elisabeth had long feared for your life, as you were away at war. She knew that the Turks had put a great price on your head.

"Then this morning—only hours ago—an arrow flew in through her window. A message was fixed to it. We now know it must have been a Turkish trick—the message reported you were killed. We could not stop her . . . her last words . . ." Father Chesare seemed unable to go on.

"Her last words." Dracula stood unmoving; his own words issued in a terrible whisper. "Tell me!"

"She left a note. It said: 'My prince is dead. All is lost without him. May God unite us in heaven.' "

"God? God!" It was a roaring challenge, hurled at the chapel ceiling. The people in the semicircle, who had tentatively begun to edge closer to their prince, now recoiled at once, as if they feared the lightning that might flash instantly to strike him down.

But then Dracula seemed, for a moment, to have forgotten God. Dropping his anguished gaze once more to the dead Elisabeth, he was struck by an oddity in her appearance.

"Why is she—like this? All wet, bloody . . . Why have her women not seen to it that she is decently prepared?"

Once more in the chapel the terrible silence reigned, now charged as with electricity.

Inevitably the burden of explanation fell to Chesare.

"My son, her women, in their misguided loyalty, were hoping to lay her to rest quickly, here in the chapel, before—" The monk stopped there, as if afraid or uncertain how to proceed.

"Yes? Yes? Before what?"

No answer. Chesare's face was pale.

"Damn you, priest, tell me!"

With great reluctance Father Chesare continued: "She has taken her own life, my son. And of course a suicide may not be buried here in consecrated ground. The women were hoping to conclude the burial in secret, before I, or any other representative of the Church—"

"The Church would refuse her sacred burial?"

"Prince, it is not my choice!" The priest was suddenly almost incoherent in his fear. "Her soul cannot be saved. She is damned. It is God's law. . . ."

Again Prince Dracula cried out wordlessly, deadly rage blended with the scream of a dying animal. Bending his lean but powerful body, he grappled with a massive stone font of holy water that stood near the low stairs and, with the strength of fury, tipped the great weight over. A surge of clear liquid overwhelmed the small puddles of river water, and washed on, reddened by Elisabeth's fresh blood, across the floor of the chapel, splashing the sandaled feet of the hastily retreating monks.

But they were not to be allowed to leave in peace. The furious lord of the castle was advancing on them.

"God's law, you say? Is this to be my reward for defending Christ's holy church? For slaying ten thousand of his enemies? Then to hell with God's law!"

A long moan of fear went up from the onlookers. Father Chesare went stumbling backward in his long robes, emitting wordless whimpers in his terror, afraid even more of the blasphemy than of the man before him. In a trembling hand Chesare raised a small wooden cross, as he might have done to defend himself against Satan himself.

The prince reached out and seized, in a grip of iron, the wrist of the arm that seemed to threaten him with the crucifix.

"Sacrilege!" the monk screamed. "Do not turn your back on Christ! Do not—" The words dissolved in a shriek of pain. The monk's arm was being bent near breaking.

The voice of Dracula was loud and clear. "I renounce God— and all you hypocrites who feed off Him. If my beloved must burn in hell—then so shall I!"

In the next instant a bone in Father Chesare's arm snapped under the pressure of that terrible grip, and the priest collapsed to his knees, emitting a mortal cry of fear and agony, even as the small cross fell from his hand to splash and clatter on the puddled floor.

It seemed that Dracula had already forgotten him. The warrior shouted: "If God would not save her, then to avenge her I will give myself to the powers of darkness!" He spread his arms and roared out: *"Let death be my life!"*

Again a groan of terror went up from those who watched and listened. There was wild alarm in the chapel, people jamming the doorway in an effort to get out.

Drawing his sword, Dracula turned and charged straight at the great wooden cross atop the altar. With all his furious strength he thrust straight for its center. The wooden symbol shivered under the piercing impact; had any human figure been there, in the position of the Crucified, it would have been impaled near the heart.

First one voice, then another, and another, screamed out that the cross was bleeding from its wound.

The chapel was filled now with a howling mob. Candles and statues were being overturned by people struggling to escape. In the confusion some even stumbled on and trampled the body of the dead woman, and many were later to report that they had seen Christ's blood now mingled on the floor with hers.

The prince, insane with grief and rage, had bounded across the sanctuary to the tabernacle that housed the Blessed Sacrament. Wrenching open the gold doors of the small chamber, he reached inside. His hand emerged gripping the golden communion chalice, whose sacred contents he dashed violently, brutally aside.

Then, springing once more to the side of Elisabeth, he bent to rake the golden goblet through the deepest puddle of bloody holy water. When he had scooped a mouthful into the cup, he raised it high.

" 'The blood is the life,' " he heard himself quoting, from sacred scripture. "And it shall be mine!"

Prince Dracula drank deep.

And with that draft it seemed to him that he was dying.

His was a terrible dying, that went unceasingly on and on.

**1**

On another sunny spring day more than four hundred years later, and a thousand miles from Castle Dracula, Mina Murray, just twenty years old, had arrived for a long visit at Hillingham House, an impressive estate in suburban London. Only a few hours had passed since the door of the guest room had closed behind the last servant helping the young guest to settle in.

A soft May breeze, laden with the scent of flowers, drifted in through Mina's opened windows, stirring her raven hair as she sat thoughtfully at a table. Her room was of a good size, in keeping with the rest of the house, and cheerfully decorated. It had been quiet until a few minutes ago, but now the peace of the afternoon was broken by the rough, staccato sound of a primitive typewriter, driven by the fingers of an energetic if not yet truly expert typist.

> 9 May, 1897. I arrived today, and shall be staying with Lucy for some weeks. The life of an assistant schoolmistress is somewhat trying, and I have longed to be with my friend, where we can talk together freely, and build our castles in the air.

Mina paused to consider. Then she typed on.

> Lucy and I have told each other all our secrets since I first tutored her at Mrs. Whitehill's school. And now we dream of being married together.
>
> Of course, when Jonathan and I are married, I shall be able to be useful to him, particularly if I can stenograph well enough to take down what he wants to say, and write it out for him on the typewriter at which I am also practicing very hard.

Having come this far with scarcely a hesitation, Mina allowed her energetic fingers to pause. Her smooth forehead creased in a slight frown, disturbing the classic beauty of her face.

"But," she murmured to herself. "It ought to be more—realistic—more businesslike—yes, if I am to be of much help as a solicitor's wife, I must strive to be businesslike!—if I type someone else's words rather than my own."

She considered a moment, looking about for suitable written or printed material, chewing her full red lower lip and frowning. Then, after a hasty and faintly guilty glance around the room, to assure herself that she was quite alone, she opened a drawer in her desk and took out a book: it was a special leatherbound edition of Sir Richard Burton's *The Thousand and One Nights*.

The edition was special in that it contained a number of illustrations of a kind not openly distributed to the public; and the picture that happened to lie on the page where the book fell open caught at Mina's attention forcibly enough to delay the resumption of typing practice.

Her dark eyes went wide, then narrowed. She was still holding the volume in her lap a minute later, and studying it with absorption, when she heard her name called behind her in a familiar voice.

Turning in startled confusion, Mina instinctively concealed the volume in her lap with a fold of her skirt. Then she relaxed slightly. "Lucy, you gave me a start!"

Lucy Westenra, redheaded, attractive, and pert, only a few months younger than her friend and guest, briskly entered the sitting room, raising both hands in a gesture of mock horror at the sight of the typewriter.

"Mina, really! Is your ambitious Jon Harker forcing you to waste a beautiful spring day learning that ridiculous machine instead of . . . of . . ."

The girl's imagination flagged, but only momentarily. Impish humor suddenly appeared. ". . . when he could be, well, perhaps forcing you to perform unspeakable acts of desperate passion on the parlor floor."

"Lucy!" Mina was genuinely offended, if only for a moment. "Really, you shouldn't talk about my fiancé in such a way."

"Oh, nooo?"

"No! There's more to marriage than—carnal pleasures. . . ." As

16

Mina turned in her chair and gestured the book she had been holding in her lap slid to the floor.

Lucy was startled at first, then pounced on the volume. "So I see! Spiritual values!"

Both girls burst into laughter. In a moment they were sitting companionably together on the floor, skirts spread around them, investigating the strange book.

"Wherever did you find this, dear?" Lucy demanded.

"In the study, where you suggested I pass an hour—it was on a shelf behind some other books. It caught my interest."

"Something of my late father's, I have no doubt, or my uncle's. What rogues they were. Well, I should think it might catch your interest—look!"

Lucy was pointing at another illustration. This one Mina had not had time to discover in her private reading, and it shocked her now.

"Lucy! Do you suppose that men and women—ever—really do—that?" The question was a serious one, though asked in a light tone.

Lucy shook her red curls pertly. "*I* did—only last night!"

"Fibber! You didn't!"

"Yes, I did—in my dreams."

Both girls laughed, though Mina did so only after a moment's hesitation, and her expression quickly became thoughtful again.

Her companion took her by the hand, then questioned her in half-playful entreaty. "Jonathan—measures up, as a man, doesn't he? Come on, you can tell Lucy."

Mina's eyes turned dreamy. "We've kissed, that's all, Jonathan and I. Sometimes I . . . press up to him, and he suddenly grows shy and says good night."

She smiled at her sympathetic listener. "He thinks he's too poor to marry me. He wants to buy me an expensive ring, and I try to tell him it doesn't matter."

Lucy had given up teasing for the moment and was full of sincere admiration. "Mina, you're the most splendid girl in all the world. . . . Anyone would love you."

Mina reached to squeeze her companion's hand. "And you are the one with regiments of men all falling at your feet."

"*But* not even one marriage proposal. And here I am almost twenty—practically a hag!"

The sound of a reserved masculine throat clearing, professionally discreet, made both girls look around. While Mina hastily closed the book Lucy got to her feet. "What is it, Hobbs?"

The butler's face was imperturbable, that of a man who could not conceivably have any interest in what forbidden pictures young ladies might be looking at, or what they were discussing. Balanced on the fingers of one hand he presented a silver salver bearing a visiting card.

Hobbs announced: "A young gentleman, miss. A Mr. Harker, to see Miss Murray. He is waiting in the garden."

Mina was astonished, pleased, and concerned all at once.

"Jonathan, here?" Murmuring something incoherent in the nature of an excuse, she hurried from the room.

From the wide side terrace of Hillingham an enormous stretch of lawn rolled in a gradual decline toward the broad Thames. The calm expanse of river today was marked with the distant sails of a few small pleasure boats. Much nearer at hand, a pair of peacocks stalked majestically upon the well-kept grass. A garden maze, contrived of tall yew hedges a century old and more, occupied a half acre below the terrace. Adjoining the maze, the family cemetery formed a pleasant and unobtrusive part of the view encompassing the entire parklike grounds.

A nervously energetic young man only a few years older than Mina, fashionably dressed as if for business in the City, was standing in the formal garden, attempting with much good humor but little success to catch a butterfly in his tall top hat. He turned expectantly at the sound of Mina's footsteps hurrying toward him, and his handsome face lit up at the sight of her.

"Jonathan, what are you doing here?" she demanded in surprise, even as she ran into his waiting arms.

Upon being greeted with a proper kiss, she recoiled, though only slightly.

'You've been drinking, in the middle of the day?" Mina knew that was not at all her fiancé's habit.

Jonathan Harker threw his arms wide again, almost losing control of his tall hat in the process.

"Quite drunk, my love, but only with success! And that's fine talk from a man's wife-to-be. You're in the company of a future partner in the firm of Hawkins and Thompkins." With darting gestures he sketched an imaginary signboard in the air. "Hawkins,

Thompkins, and Harker—that has a fine sound to it, don't you think?"

"Jonathan! A partnership?" Mina's red lips went round and wide. "How marvelous!"

Harker sobered a trifle. "The truth is that my erstwhile superior and rival for promotion, Mr. Renfield, has finally lost his greedy mind—and I've been promoted in his place."

Only the fact of the promotion, and not the unhappy circumstance that had made it possible, really registered in the young woman's thought. Again she flung herself into her fiancé's arms.

"Oh, Jonathan, I'm so happy for you! Why, this means that we don't have to wait. Doesn't it? Doesn't it? We can be married right away—I must tell Lucy—when shall we be married? When?"

Harker put on his hat, that he might have both hands free to hold her fondly by arms and shoulders. "As soon as I return."

"Return?" Mina was startled anew. "From where?"

"I'm off, this very day, to exotic Eastern Europe. Some business Mr. Renfield's illness prevented his concluding."

"Tell me all about it."

Linking arms with Mina, Harker began to stroll with her about the garden. Their feet kept more or less automatically to the manicured paths, and from time to time he patted her small hand resting on his forearm. Peacocks screamed out eerie cries before them.

Harker said: "Some nobleman in the exotic wilds of Transylvania is acquiring property—a number of properties—around London, and I am being sent to close the transactions. Money is no object, and our legal fees will be substantial, to say the least. Extraordinary. Can you imagine the power that sort of wealth commands? Think of it, Mina!"

"I'm thinking of our wedding, Jon."

"As I say, we shall be able to be married as soon as I return— now we can make it a grand, expensive affair, that Lucy and all her aristocratic friends will talk about."

Their stroll had brought them near the entrance to the maze of tall yew hedge. Mina stopped, staring into the beginning of the shaded pathway. She said: "I don't really care about them—how they talk. I just want us to be happy—don't you see?"

Her companion was gazing at her fondly. "And we *shall* be happy, my little nightingale—I know what's best, for both of us."

"Of course." A small cloud seemed to have come over the sun. "We've waited so long—haven't we?"

This raising, however obliquely, of the subject of time, caused Harker to drop Mina's arm and dig into his waistcoat pocket for his watch. His eyebrows went up.

"I hadn't realized. . . . Darling, I *must* dash. You aren't to worry, now. I'll write faithfully—"

"Jonathan, I love you!" And Mina surprised them both with the ferocity of her kiss.

It was a kiss that Harker looked back on with fond longing a week later. During the seven days since his departure from London the young solicitor had been almost continually aboard one train or another, and by this time had put many weary railway miles behind him, inhaling a great deal of coal smoke in the process.

His current transportation was a section of the famed Orient Express, which he had ridden from Paris east through Budapest, and which was now bearing him even farther toward the rising sun. The final destination of this train—though Harker did not intend to stay with it that far—was the Bulgarian Black Sea port of Varna.

So far Harker had found the journey tiring, but far from boring. The alterations in customs, language, and scenery that he had encountered had already been more than enough to convince him that he had definitely left the more or less familiar peoples and places of Western Europe far behind.

Harker had foresightedly equipped himself for his trip with several maps, as well as guidebooks and railroad timetables, and had found them very useful. Though for days now his maps had remained almost continually folded in his pockets, he had already studied them sufficiently that in his mind's eye he could visualize in satisfactory detail what they had to say regarding the region he was about to enter.

The district in which his rather mysterious client resided was in the extreme east of the territory known as Transylvania—which meant, of course, "The Land Beyond the Forest." One of the guidebooks consulted by the young solicitor had assured him that every known superstition in the world was gathered into the horseshoe of the Carpathians, as if it were the center of some sort of imaginative whirlpool; Harker had an idea that this might make his stay interesting, and planned to ask Count Dracula about some of the more exotic local beliefs.

All during the seventh day of his journey the train seemed to dawdle through a country that impressed the traveler as being full of beauty of every kind. Sometimes little towns or castles appeared on the top of steep hills; sometimes the rails closely followed the course of rivers and streams, which seemed from the wide stony margin on each side to be subject to great floods. At every station, large and small, were groups of people, sometimes crowds, in all sorts of attire. Some reminded Harker of the peasants of France or Germany, with short jackets and round hats and homemade trousers; others he considered very picturesque. He considered the strangest to be the Slovaks, who struck the English visitor as more barbarian than the rest, with big cowboy hats, baggy trousers of dirty white, white linen shirts, and enormous heavy leather belts, nearly a foot wide, and all studded over with brass nails.

One item of equipment now very often out of the young traveler's pocket and in his hands was the neat notebook in which Harker had determined to keep a day-to-day, and sometimes hour-by-hour, journal of this interesting trip. He looked forward with keen anticipation to being able to share it all with Mina.

His latest entry read:

> The region which is my destination lies on the borders of three states, Transylvania, Moldavia, and Bukovina, in the midst of the Carpathian Mountains—to an ordinary Englishman like myself one of the wildest and least-known portions of Europe.

The railroad could carry Harker no closer to his goal than a town called Bistritz, of some twelve thousand inhabitants, and upon his arrival there in late afternoon he left the train. The place was certainly picturesque enough to suit him, surrounded as it was by the ruins of antique fortifications; and Harker was pleased to find that in accordance with Count Dracula's meticulous instructions, a room had been reserved for him at the Golden Krone Hotel.

When he registered at the Golden Krone, the young solicitor was immediately handed a letter from his client, written in a neat English script:

> My friend—Welcome to the Carpathians. I am anxiously expecting you. Sleep well tonight. At three tomorrow the diligence will start for Bukovina; a place on it is kept for you. At the Borgo Pass my

carriage will await you and will bring you on to me. I trust that your journey from London has been a happy one, and that you will enjoy your stay in my beautiful land.

Your friend,
Dracula

Harker lay fitfully in his bed at the Golden Krone, but he had dined well, and if his food came more heavily seasoned with pepper and paprika than he was accustomed to, he was ready to accept this and other peculiarities of the place in a spirit of adventure.

For breakfast on the next day he had more paprika, as seasoning in a sort of porridge of maize flour, with eggplant. After breakfast he passed the time agreeably enough in making and noting observations of things that interested him.

When, in midafternoon, it came time to board the coach, the traveler was interested to discover that his only companions were a taciturn local merchant and two Gypsy women, the latter apparently mother and daughter. As far as Harker could make out, none of the three spoke English, or any other language with which he had the least familiarity.

All three of these natives, when they learned that the young foreigner's destination was the Borgo Pass, gazed at him with odd expressions, compounded of what he took to be pity and alarm. This attitude Harker found somewhat unsettling—as he did the proximity of the voluptuous young Gypsy woman, who happened to be seated across from him, and whose knee touched his from time to time in the close confines of the coach.

The ride began uneventfully enough, though the driver kept the horses at a swifter pace than Harker had expected. At intervals during the journey his fellow passengers conversed among themselves in a language he could not begin to understand, exchanging some remarks that Harker was convinced referred to him.

The four had been confined together for several hours in the vehicle, swaying and bouncing over gradually deteriorating roads, and Harker was using the last of the fading daylight to yearn over a small metal-framed photograph of Mina, when suddenly the young Gypsy woman, who had been studying the foreigner intently for some time, appeared to come to a decision.

Leaning forward boldly, and smiling as if in reassurance, she seized Harker's right hand. He hastily used his free hand to stuff Mina's picture into one of his pockets, and was about to attempt to convey to the Gypsy that he had no wish to have his fortune told, when he realized that the young woman's object had rather been to give him something.

Looking down, totally at a loss to understand, he observed the object the girl had pressed into his hand—it was a small crucifix, attached to a fine chain that appeared to be of silver.

The two women, with energetic signs and coaxings, were making plain to Harker their urgent desire that he should put the silver chain around his neck. When Harker looked helplessly to the merchant, that gentleman, chewing his heavy mustache, only frowned and nodded thoughtfully, as if he thought that on the whole what the women were suggesting was a good idea.

Willing to make an effort to humor his traveling companions, Harker took off his hat and slipped the thin chain over his head. Immediately the two women were all smiles and satisfaction—yes, there was no doubt that was really what they had wanted him to do. He put on his hat again and sat back.

The vague mental discomfort that Harker would ordinarily have expected to experience upon submitting to this popish and vaguely idolatrous custom for some reason failed to materialize. Instead he found the touch of the silver image—well, rather comforting.

He decided he would note it in those words, at the next opportunity he had of writing in his journal.

"Thank you," he said, bobbing his head rather formally to each of the women in turn. "Thank you."

And he thought that perhaps, though they could understand no English, his smile and gestures managed to convey his meaning. The women, as he thought, gave every sign of satisfaction with his behavior, but none that (as Harker had more than half expected) any form of payment was required from him.

Presently the sun was gone, its last rays turning pink the snowy eastern mountaintops; and at its disappearance the driver stopped, briefly, to light the coach's lanterns against the fall of night. Then he resumed his high seat, and his whip again cracked sharply in the briskly chilling air, urging on the horses to maintain their speed despite the evident poorness and increasing steepness of the road.

The next stop, according to the instructions Harker had received from his client, should be the Borgo Pass.

In the darkness the road was no longer visible to the passengers, but the jolting of the coach testified that it must have deteriorated further. To the English traveler, the hours of the night seemed endless. The lanterns burning on the outside of the coach gave only feeble light. The moon remained for long minutes at a time behind scudding clouds, emerging rarely to hint at mountainous terrain, partially wooded and partly desolate, without, as far as Harker could discern, the light of a single farm or village for many miles.

Then suddenly, and quite unexpectedly as far as Harker was concerned, the driver was pulling his hard-worked horses to a stop. Peering from the window of the coach, Harker could dimly perceive that they had arrived at a clearing of some kind, a widening of the road as if at a fork or resting place, though no alternate track was readily discernible. Some kind of roadside shrine, as he thought it, was visible; vaguely in the silent darkness he could perceive what looked like a giant crucifix.

Harker was reasonably sure that the driver spoke at least a little English. Clearing his throat, he called out the window: "Is this—I say, is this the place? I . . ."

Harker received no answer, but evidently it was the place where he was to be met, or at least the driver had determined that it was, for the man had scrambled from his seat atop the coach and was hurriedly unstrapping Harker's trunk. In another moment his entire baggage had been rudely, crudely thrown to the ground.

This brought a cry of outrage from the owner. "You there! You ought to be careful. . . ."

But to protest seemed completely useless. And now the driver, his face grim, moving as if moments for some reason counted, was holding the door open for Harker, urgently beckoning him out.

On alighting from the coach, Harker looked around, hoping to catch sight of the conveyance which was to take him to the count. Each moment he expected to see the glaze of approaching lamps through the blackness, but nothing of the kind appeared. The only light was the flickering rays of the lamps of the vehicle in which he had been riding. In that illumination the steam from the hard-driven horses rose in a white cloud. He could now see the white sandy road lying ahead, but on it was no sign of a vehicle.

Getting out of doors at least made it possible for him to stretch his cramped legs, and to read his watch, by bringing it near one of the flaring coach lanterns.

"We are early!" Harker protested, staring, blinking at the dial, then holding the instrument to his ear. If his watch was correct—and the timepiece seemed to be ticking along as evenly as ever—the steaming horses had brought him to Borgo Pass a full hour ahead of schedule.

Again he endeavored to register a protest with the driver: "Even if this is the right place, we are an hour early, and no one is here to meet me. No . . ."

But it was futile. The merchant and the women were staring at their erstwhile companion with pity—and with relief, as if rejoicing to be rid of him. Then the door of the coach banged shut; and the driver, when Harker looked for him again, was already back on his high seat, picking up his whip.

A few moments after that, and as far as the young traveler from England could tell, he seemed to have the night and the high Carpathians all to himself. There was only the fading rumble of coach wheels, diminishing hoofbeats, the snap of a whip. Even running an hour ahead of schedule as they were, obviously neither driver nor passengers had been minded to dally in these parts a minute longer than was absolutely necessary—

And what was *that*? Harker asked himself, turning his head suddenly to listen.

Had it really been a wolf's howl? In a country so wild, a world away from suburban London, he could well believe it.

The faint faraway wailing noise was repeated, then answered from somewhere rather uncomfortably near at hand. Unconsciously the solicitor found himself moving away from his dumped heavy baggage, moving toward the vaguely visible shrine or signpost, as if by so doing he might somehow cling to the nearest vestige of civilization, a sign that humanity indeed retained some foothold in this world.

Then it occurred to Harker that possibly a signpost might be helpful in some practical way, if he had been let out in the wrong place after all, and with the coming of daylight would have to find his own way back to civilization. Of course, in this darkness any letters or numbers would be difficult to read, even if the language should be familiar, which seemed unlikely.

And in fact the thing itself, when Harker came close enough to see it at all clearly, was very strange. At all events, it was certainly no signpost.

His first impression had evidently been correct. A great cross, but oddly enough the man-sized carven figure crucified upon it was not human—or not entirely.

Tentatively he reached up and touched the legs. The wooden body was a man's, but the head appeared to be that of a wolf.

To Harker the strangest thing about the figure was that in this setting, it seemed somehow—appropriate.

Turning away from the shrine—if such it was—Harker spent a long and rather uncomfortable few minutes strolling back and forth over the same few yards of road, now and then whistling or humming to himself. He did his best to distract himself from thoughts of danger and difficulty by mentally reviewing the business he had come here to conclude. This was a fairly complex affair, involving the purchase of a number of properties.

At last, with some relief, he caught the sound of horses and a rumble of wheels approaching, this time from a direction at right angles to the road he had already traveled. By now his eyes had made a good adjustment to the darkness, and he could manage to make out the faint track of the side road. Jolting along it at a good pace came the sparks of the new vehicle's lamps.

Soon it was close enough for Harker to obtain a better look. Coal-black and splendid animals were pulling a calèche, a half-open carriage with a high coachman's seat in front.

The driver who crouched upon that seat was clad in a peculiar livery indeed, dark short cape and high collar under a black hat or helmet suggesting the head of a predatory bird. Only a portion of a pale face was left exposed.

Stopping the calèche in a position that brought his elevated perch exactly opposite the waiting passenger, the driver called down to him in guttural German: "My master the count bade me take all good care of you, *mein Herr!*"

A moment later Harker, to his vast astonishment, found himself caught by hand and shoulder, and literally lifted, swung into the half-open body of the carriage. Stunned, he could only sit for a long moment where he had been placed while the nimble coachman, giving further evidence of prodigious strength, hoisted his heavy trunk and other baggage aboard.

The young solicitor sat there, physically comfortable enough, while a heavy robe was draped efficiently around him. A flask, which by the smell of it contained slivovitz, the local plum brandy, was pressed into his hand. Then, with a crack of the whip, the final leg of his journey was under way.

And still, continually, out of the darkness surrounding the moving calèche, there sounded the hungry, mournful voices of the wolves as if the pack were following. . . . Harker barely tasted the slivovitz.

The next two hours passed in journeying even swifter than before—though this driver's whip cracked much less frequently—and eventually it seemed to Harker that even wolves had probably have been left behind. The road, even narrower now and rougher than that the coach from Bistritz had brought him on, wound and switchbacked endlessly on and up among the mountains, sometimes skirting the edge of a precipice, sometimes plunging for long minutes into a tunnel of pines. Still the darkness on every side remained utterly unrelieved by any dot of illumination from farm or Gypsy camp.

And then, without warning, the edifice that Harker knew must be his destination came into view, already startlingly close on its high promontory; it was a vast ruined castle, from whose tall black windows issued no ray of light, and whose broken battlements showed a jagged line against the moonlit sky.

A scant minute later, the calèche was rumbling under a long, low roof of stone and emerging into an open courtyard of the ancient building, half fortress and half palace.

Only moments after having entered the courtyard, Harker and his baggage were being deposited at the foot of a flight of crumbling stairs leading up to a massive door, the lintel above which had been carved into a great stone dragon arch.

Scarcely had Harker's trunk thudded down upon the moonlit pavement then the calèche was pulling away, the dark, mysteriously costumed driver snapping his whip as briskly as ever over the backs of still-energetic horses. The visiting Englishman found himself completely alone, and as bewildered as he had been at any time since leaving Paris.

Long moments passed in silence. Half-silvered by moonlight as it was, the courtyard looked to be of considerable size, and several dark ways led from it under great round arches. The door confronting the visitor showed no sign of bell or knocker, and Harker thought it unlikely that his voice would be able to penetrate through these frowning walls and dark window openings.

The time the visitor was forced to wait seemed endless, and

vague doubts and fears came crowding in upon him. What sort of grim adventure, he demanded of himself, was this on which he had embarked? Was this a customary incident in the life of a solicitor's clerk sent out to explain the purchase of London property to a foreigner?

Then, with a mental effort, Harker corrected himself. Solicitor's clerk indeed! Mina would not like that unconscious reversion to his former humble status. He was a solicitor now, and would be a partner soon, if all went well and this business could be successfully concluded—

Harker's head jerked around, as from somewhere in the ruined portion of the great castle there had reached his ears a sound as of a small rock falling. This clatter was followed by smaller noises, suggesting to the visitor that the stone might have been dislodged by the feet of a scurrying rat.

Enough of passive waiting.

The young solicitor had just, with some difficulty, gathered up his heavy baggage into his own hands, squared his shoulders, and set foot on the lowest stair, when, after a preliminary noise of rattling chains, and the clanking of massive bolts drawn back, the door at the top was suddenly opened, revealing a single figure, the shadow of a man outlined against faint interior illumination.

In a moment the man in the high doorway had raised in his right hand an antique silver lamp, whose flame burned without chimney or globe of any kind, throwing long quivering shadows as it flickered in the draft through the open door.

The figure now fully revealed was clad from neck to foot in a crimson robe. A mass of white hair was swept and combed back above a high forehead and an aged, clean-shaven face of deathly pallor. There was not a single speck of color about the head or face—except for the man's eyes, which were a cold vivid blue.

"Welcome to my house!" the old man's voice resounded. His English was excellent, though to Harker's ears the intonation was somewhat strange. "Come freely, go safely, and leave some of the happiness you bring!"

With a grunt of relief, Harker set his heavy trunk down on the stair. "Count . . . Dracula?"

With a nimbleness that belied the wrinkled pallor of his face, the man in the red robe came down the steps to meet the arriving guest, offered him a courtly bow, and in the same movement snatched up the heavy trunk with incredible ease.

"I am Dracula, and I bid you welcome, Mr. Harker, to my house. Come in; the night air is chill, and you must need to eat and rest."

Harker climbed the steps. Then, drawing a deep breath, he stepped in across the threshold.

I mmediately upon entering Dracula's house, Harker attempted to regain custody of his baggage.

But his forceful host would not permit it. "Nay, sir! You are my guest. It is late, and my people are not available. Let me see to your comfort myself."

After locking and bolting the castle's great front door, the white-haired count, carrying Harker's heavy trunk easily in one hand, and still bearing the antique lamp in the other, preceded Harker up a zigzag stair of stone.

As the young man climbed he looked about him with wonder and appreciation. The interior of the castle, of this portion of it anyway, looked much more solid in its fabric, far better kept, than the ruinous appearance of the exterior had suggested. The wavering light of the lamp in Count Dracula's hand, falling on strange statues, cast even stranger shadows on walls and ceiling, on faded tapestries and old paintings; and it drew faint gleams from mounted sets of medieval armor and edged weapons.

Once more Harker considered that as evidently no servants were available, he ought to assume the burden of his own baggage; but the manner of his host silently discouraged the attempt. Count Dracula, laden as he was, took flight after flight of stairs at a brisk, untiring pace, leaving the younger Harker puffing in an effort to keep up.

Presently, without breaking stride, the white-haired man turned his head and demanded cheerfully: "Come, tell me of the London properties you have procured for me!"

Harker, glad of his recent effort to review the business, did the best he could, while puffing.

"Well, sir, I believe the most remarkable is the estate called Carfax. No doubt the name is a corruption of the French term *quatre face*, as the house is four-sided, lined up exactly with the four points of the compass."

His host glanced back while Harker paused for breath. Then the young man continued: "There are about twenty acres, quite surrounded by a solid stone wall. There are many trees on it, which make it in places gloomy, and there is a deep, dark-looking pond.

"The house itself is quite large, and of all periods back, I should say, to medieval times, for one part is of stone immensely thick. It has not been repaired for a large number of years."

Count Dracula, who had considerately waited for him, nodded thoughtfully. They climbed on, now passing ancient Greek and Roman statues, all seemingly in perfect condition.

"I am glad that it is old," the count remarked at last. "I come from an old family, and to live in a new house would kill me."

The young visitor was much relieved to be shown at last into a well-lit room in which a table was spread for supper—there was only a single place setting, of golden plates and goblets along with covered serving dishes; antique work that, as Harker quickly estimated, must have been worth a small fortune. On this room's mighty hearth a great fire of logs, recently replenished, flamed and flared, driving away the chill of the Carpathian night. Here, as in the other portions of the castle the visitor had so far seen, weapons formed a large part of the wall decorations.

The count closed the door by which they had entered from the corridor, then, crossing the room, opened another door, which led into a snug bedroom, invitingly well lighted and warmed with another log fire, which sent a hollow roar up the wide chimney.

Here he put down Harker's bags and withdrew, saying: "You will need to refresh yourself after your journey. When you are ready, come into the other room, where you will find your supper prepared."

The light and warmth of these rooms, and his host's courteous welcome, had already gone far to dissipate Harker's fears, and the young man realized that he was half-famished. He quickly did as he had been bidden.

On returning to the sitting room, he found Count Dracula leaning against the stonework of the great fireplace. Dracula indicated the table with a graceful wave of his hand.

"I pray you," he urged his guest, "be seated and sup how you please. You will, I trust, excuse me that I do not join you; but I have dined already, and I do not sup."

Even as the count spoke he stepped forward and himself took the cover off a dish, revealing an excellent roast chicken. There were also, as Harker soon discovered, cheese, and salad, and a dusty bottle of aromatic old Tokay.

Harker fell to at once. Conversation, while he ate and drank—rationing himself to two glasses of the enjoyable wine—ranged over some of the unusual things he had observed on his journey. Dracula remained standing beside the fireplace, evidently quite comfortable in that position. He listened with interest to Harker's remarks and was able to explain some of the events and customs the Englishman had found puzzling.

As soon as Harker had finished eating, he arose and accepted a cigar offered by his host, then lighted it with a splinter of wood plucked from the hearth.

A faint sound from outside the window made the visitor turn in that direction, where he was able to observe the first dim streak of the coming dawn. To Harker there seemed, at this moment, a strange, fresh stillness over everything; but as he listened he heard once more, as if from the valley below the castle, the howling of many wolves.

His host's eyes gleamed at the sound. Quietly the old man remarked: "Listen to them—the children of the night! What music they make!"

Harker, doing his best to be polite but feeling very sleepy, murmured something.

The count smiled knowingly at the young foreigner's lack of comprehension. "We are in Transylvania; and Transylvania is not England. Our ways are not your ways, and there shall be to you many strange things. This ground was fought over for centuries, by my ancestors against the Saxon and the Turk. There is hardly a foot of soil in all this region that has not been enriched by the blood of patriots and invaders!"

He paused, then added in a quieter voice: "You may go anywhere you wish in the castle, except where the doors are locked, where of course you will not wish to go."

"I am sure of it, sir. . . ." Harker paused, his curiosity aroused, blinking away sleep. "Count Dracula, that face in the tapestry behind you . . . an ancestor, perhaps? I believe I detect a resemblance . . . ?"

"Ha, yes." The old man turned his head and appeared to consider the figures in the tapestry with satisfaction. "The Order of the Dragon. An ancient society, pledging my forefathers to defend the Church against all enemies."

Turning back to Harker, the count displayed white pointed teeth. "Alas, the relationship was not entirely . . . successful."

Harker blinked at him, not sure that he had understood what the words and the wicked smile seemed to imply. "They were, I am sure, good Christians, even as you—"

"We are Draculas!" the count roared, and his eyes seemed to glow red. In the next instant he had snatched down one of the weapons from the wall, a curved Turkish sword.

He brandished the blade in his right hand. "And we Draculas have a right to be proud! Is it a wonder we are a conquering race? What devil or witch was ever so great as Attila, whose blood flows in these veins?"

He slashed the air with the sword, right and left, so that Harker, shaken, his cigar forgotten, recoiled. Then Dracula used the curved blade as a pointer, emphatically indicating the proud face of the warlord in the tapestry. "His glory is my glory!"

As abruptly as it had appeared, the burst of demonic energy faded. The old man's shoulders slumped and he reached tiredly to restore the weapon to its sheath upon the wall.

Gazing into the distance, he said, in a much softer voice: "Blood is too precious a thing in these times. And the glories of my great race are as a tale that is told."

Turning slowly, drained, saddened, no longer frightful, he approached Harker. He added: "I am the last of my kind."

Harker bowed, somewhat stiffly following his shock. At least he was no longer having to struggle to stay awake. "I have offended you with my ignorance, Count. Forgive me."

Dracula bowed in turn, accepting the apology. "Forgive *me*, my young friend. It is long since I have been accustomed to guests. And I am weary with many years of mourning over the dead."

But already a relentless energy was driving back the appearance of age and weariness. A kind of smile returned to the count's face.

"Your employer, Mr. Hawkins, writes most highly of your talents. Come, tell me more of the houses you have procured for me!"

* * *

Half an hour later, the conference between purchaser and agent had been adjourned to another well-lighted room, where a number of documents, including deeds and legal descriptions, had been set out on a broad table. Overlooking the table was a large-scale wall map of London and its vicinity; Harker had just finished pinning several photographs to this map, pictures showing some of the various properties Dracula had just purchased through his solicitors, and which were indicated on the map by red circles in ten locations.

Dracula, using an antique quill pen and a pot of ink, was just signing the last paper required of him.

As he did so he was saying: "I do so long to go through the crowded streets of your mighty London, to be in the midst of the whirl and rush of humanity, to share its life, its change—its death—"

On that final word he pushed the completed deed across to Harker, who folded it and applied a seal of hot wax.

"There. You, Count, are now the owner of the estate called Carfax, at Purfleet."

Moving to the wall map, the young solicitor indicated one of the photographs he had just tacked up. This one showed an ancient house of stone.

Dracula nodded.

Harker turned back to the table, where some additional photographs, not yet mounted, lay mixed up with the other paperwork.

"I've also brought pictures of some of the other houses—forgive my curiosity, sir, but as your solicitor in London, it may be helpful for me to know—why purchase ten houses, distributed around the city? Is this some strategy of investment, intended to increase the market value of all the properties? Or—"

Dracula meanwhile had drawn closer to the table; and on happening to look down from the wall map, he saw something there, immediately before him, that froze him almost motionless.

A single spasmodic movement of his hand, involuntary reaction to tremendous shock, upset the inkpot, sending a great stain, reddish brown like drying blood, rushing across the table's surface.

The count's hand, pointy-nailed and abnormally hairy on the palm, moved much more swiftly than the spill, to rescue one object from the spreading ink and hold it up.

Harker, gazing into the man's face, was astonished once again— it seemed to him for a moment that he was looking at a corpse.

Such was the intensity of Dracula's concentration upon the photograph now in his hand.

The count's lips moved, and a whispering, altered voice came forth.

"The luckiest man who walks on this earth is one who finds—true love." And now, at last, he raised his compelling blue eyes from the picture to gaze at Harker.

That young man, in some confusion over this latest turn of events, stared at the photograph in puzzlement, and then conducted a rapid search of his own inner pockets.

"Ah—I see you have found—Mina. I had thought she was lost, but somehow her picture must have got in among the other photographs. We are to be married, as soon as I return to England."

Even as he uttered those last words Harker suddenly turned his head, squinting at the room's open door, beyond which lay a dark hallway. For a moment it had seemed to the young man that he had heard, almost unimaginably faint, the rustle of feminine garments, the sound of women's laughter.

But perhaps the sound had been only an illusion, a trick of wind, or of mice squealing and scampering in the old walls. Certainly Dracula gave no sign of being aware of any other presence. He set down Mina's photo, carefully choosing a dry spot on the table.

Feeling the need to make conversation, Harker inquired: "Sir, are you married?"

The count was still staring at Mina's picture, and the answer was slow in coming.

"I was . . . ages ago, it seems. Unfortunately she died."

"I'm very sorry."

"But perhaps she was fortunate. My life at its best is . . . misery." Carefully picking up the photograph of Mina once again, he handed it over to Harker. "She will no doubt make a devoted wife."

Harker, murmuring something awkward in the way of an acknowledgment, replaced the image where it belonged, deep in an inner pocket of his coat.

Dracula, briskly rubbing his hands together, was suddenly all business. "And now, my dear young friend, it would be good if you would write some letters. It will doubtless please your friends to know that you are well, and that you look forward to getting home to them."

"Sir?"

"Write now, if you please. Two letters at least, I think. One to your future partner Mr. Hawkins; another to . . . any loved ones you may have. Say that you shall stay with me until a month from now."

The young solicitor was taken aback and had to struggle to keep from showing his disappointment openly. Lamely he asked: "Do you wish me to stay so long?"

"I desire it much." The strange blue eyes grew very hard. "Nay, I will take no refusal. There is much I would have you tell me— about London. About England and all her people."

Taking note of his visitor's continued reluctance, the count persevered. "And when your master, employer—call Mr. Hawkins what you will—engaged that someone should come here on his behalf, it was understood that my needs only were to be consulted. I have not stinted. Is it not so?"

The sharp-nailed hand pushed forward on the table several sheets of writing paper and envelopes; Harker took note that all were of the thinnest foreign post. Whatever he might write on them could easily be read, even after the envelopes were sealed.

Still he felt he could do nothing, in the circumstances, but bow his acceptance.

Dracula smiled; once more he was all graciousness. "But you must be tired. I am remiss as a host; your bedroom is all in readiness, and tomorrow you shall sleep as late as you will. I have to be away until the afternoon; so sleep well and dream well!"

And Harker retired, noting in his journal that he found himself "all in a sea of wonders. I doubt; I fear; I think strange things which I dare not confess to my own soul. God keep me, if only for the sake of those dear to me!"

Having slept for a few hours, rather uneasily though without any obvious cause of disturbance, Harker awoke to bright sunlight coming in. He got up, and gazed for a time at the empty, utterly deserted, half-ruined courtyard beneath the windows of his rooms. Here and there weeds grew through the pavement, and dust had drifted into all the corners. The archway built and carved into a dragon's shape seemed an enigma worthy of comparison to the Sphinx.

All was quiet in the hallway outside Harker's door and, indeed, throughout the whole castle, as far as he could tell; never yet had he seen or heard any movement or talk of servants.

He washed, and dressed himself, and returned to the room where he had supped the night before. There he found a cold breakfast laid out, with coffee kept hot by the pot being placed on the hearth.

On the table was a card, bearing a message in Dracula's hand:

I have to be absent for a while. Do not wait for me.

—D.

Harker was, as he thought, rapidly becoming accustomed to oddities. He fell to and enjoyed a hearty meal. When he had done, he looked for a bell, that he might let the servants know that he had finished; but he could not find one.

Pouring himself more coffee, he sat for a while considering the odd deficiencies in the house, which contrasted so sharply with the extraordinary evidences of wealth. At this meal the table service was again of gold, so beautifully wrought that Harker thought it must be of immense value. The curtains and upholstery of the chairs and sofas in both his rooms, and the hangings of the bed, were of the costliest and most beautiful fabrics. They were centuries old, Harker thought, having seen something like them in the old palace at Hampton Court.

But there were certainly peculiarities. For example, in none of the rooms that he had seen so far was there even the simplest mirror; it seemed he would have to get out the little shaving glass from his bag before he could either shave or brush his hair.

Even stranger, he had not yet seen a servant anywhere, or heard a human voice or movement, other than his own or Dracula's, near the castle. There were only occasional bird songs, and the howling of wolves, to accompany the intermittent moaning of the wind around the windows and the battlements.

Having finished his coffee, Harker wrote the letters his host had requested and sealed them in their envelopes—where, he observed, they were as transparently readable as he had expected.

That task accomplished, he looked about for something to read—he did not like to set out attempting to explore the castle without the count's express permission.

His own rooms contained absolutely nothing in the way of books or newspapers; going out into the hall and tentatively trying another door, he was pleased to discover a sizable library, neatly kept and furnished.

And in the library, to Harker's great delight, were a vast number of English books, whole shelves full of them, and bound volumes of magazines and newspapers. The place had a pleasant air of use and occupation. A table in the center was littered with English magazines and newspapers, though none of very recent date.

The books were of the most varied kind—history, geography, politics, botany, geology, law—all relating to England and English life and customs and manners.

After spending a pleasant hour or so in the library, Harker returned to his own quarters. There he entered an account of his recent experiences and impressions in his journal, which he was still determined to keep as faithfully as possible.

11 May. I began to fear as I wrote in this book that I was getting too diffuse; but now I am glad that I went into detail from the first, for there is something so strange about this place and all in it that I cannot but feel uneasy. I wish I were safe out of it, and that I had never come. It may be that this strange night existence is telling on me; but would that were all! If there were anyone to talk to, I could bear it, but there is no one. I have only the count to speak with, and he

Harker broke off at that point, unable or unwilling to set down his own half-formed fears and notions.

Having again sought unsuccessfully in the apartment for a mirror of any kind, he brought out his own small shaving mirror from his trunk and hung it near the window, where the light was best. Realizing that it would be pointless to try to summon a servant, he built up the smoldering fire a little himself and put a pan of water on the hearth to heat.

Harker got out his straight razor, honed the edge rhythmically on the short leather strop, and presently began to shave, humming lightly to himself a tune from Gilbert and Sullivan. Bright sunshine, chirping sparrows near his window, and the sense of having successfully concluded an unusual item of business, combined to drive away vague terrors and apprehensions.

He told himself that last night many things—the strangeness of the journey, the wolves, the peculiarities of his eccentric client— had combined to have a strong effect upon his nerves. But this morning he felt that he had put all such dreams and vapors behind him.

Small wonder, though, Harker mused to himself, that his predecessor, poor Renfield, had suffered seriously from his journey to these regions. Harker wasn't sure whether Renfield had actually stayed at Castle Dracula, or had even reached it—he would have to ask his host about that. But any man with the least tendency toward—well, toward instability—on being subjected to such strains—

"Good morning."

The words were spoken so close behind Harker, so distinctly uttered in the middle of a room shown by the shaving mirror to be completely devoid of other people, that the young man could not repress a start as he whirled around. The razor in his hand inevitably inflicted a small nick on his chin.

Count Dracula, garbed as on the previous night, his face fixed in a faint smile, was standing little more than an arm's length behind him.

Muttering some kind of response to the salutation, Harker involuntarily turned back, wondering, to the shaving glass. His eyes and brain confirmed the incredible fact that the mirror presented no image at all of his visitor, though every other object in the room was plainly reflected.

Obviously his host was aware of his confusion. But it was equally obvious that no explanation was going to be offered.

"Take care!" warned Dracula, demonstrating a sudden anger. "Take care how you cut yourself! In this country it is more dangerous than you think!"

The count stepped forward, causing his young guest to recoil involuntarily.

"And this is the wretched thing that has done the mischief! It is a foul bauble of man's vanity. Away with it!" Harker, later trying to remember exactly what happened in the next moment, could never be quite sure. It seemed to him that Dracula had never actually touched the little mirror, but that the glass warped and distorted of itself, and in another instant broke, sending a spray of sharp bright fragments onto the carpet.

While Harker stood stunned, the count, moving calmly and deliberately, plucked the razor from the young man's almost nerveless hand. Harker saw him turn his back and raise his hands toward his own face—and the count's red-sleeved arms and shoulder moved with a spasmodic shudder.

Turning once more to face Harker, Dracula was still for a moment, poised in the pose of a barber—or an assassin—right hand still clutching the bright steel. Dimly Harker, who had momentarily ceased to breathe, noted that the blade had been wiped clean—somehow—of lather and of the trace of blood.

Dracula licked his red lips. Then, as if suddenly remembering something, the old man demanded: "The letters I requested—have you written them?"

The young man gasped. "Yes, sir—they are on the table."

"Good."

With a motion of his chin and hand Dracula indicated that Harker should remain still; then with a gentle motion of his left hand under Harker's chin, he tilted up his half-shaven face into the full light of the open window.

The sharpness of the razor approached the cheek that was still lathered and unshaven; the steel edge caressed the skin there delicately and efficiently—a movement under exquisitely precise control.

Meanwhile Harker remained in exactly the position where he had been posed; it seemed to him that his body knew it must not move a fraction of an inch, that it dared not even quiver with the fear that was making his heart pound.

A razor, in the hand of a madman, of a monster . . .

Another delicate stroke of steel, removing nothing but whiskers and lather. And yet another gentle stroke. Abstractedly, seeming to concentrate his entire attention on the job of shaving, the count spoke in a kind of monotone, as if he were only musing aloud.

"Let me advise you, my dear young friend . . . nay, let me warn you, with all seriousness . . . should you leave these rooms, you will not by chance go to sleep in any other part of the castle. It is old, and has many memories . . . and there are bad dreams for those who sleep unwisely. . . ."

The old man's voice trailed off. Harker could see that Dracula's burning eyes were fixed on his throat, or rather just below it—on the place where the Gypsy's rosary must now be visible under his collar, which was opened now for shaving.

"I'm sure I understand," Harker heard himself whispering. "I have seen—strange things here already."

But perhaps the count did not hear this remark, for he had

already turned away, leaving the job of shaving still incomplete. The razor, this time unwiped, suddenly lay on the table where the three letters were no longer; and the room's thick door slammed shut with a heavy sound, which seemed to bear a burden of finality.

This evening the great hall at Hillingham was coming alive with conversation and subdued laughter—a harpist, having tuned up, was beginning to play tunes from the latest Gilbert and Sullivan operetta. One carriage after another was pulling in along the great curving drive, stopping to discharge elegantly dressed guests, then pulling away again to wait for their departure.

Near the middle of the hall a frail, gray-haired woman, elegantly gowned, stood greeting the succession of arriving guests. This was Mrs. Westenra, Lucy's widowed mother and owner of the estate. Mrs. Westenra's health had been poor for a long time, and between arrivals she rested on a divan, fanning herself.

Mina had finished dressing for the party and had come out of her room, but she had not yet joined the small throng below. Instead she lingered reluctantly on the top landing of the main stair, observing below the gaiety so much out of tune with her own feelings.

In the days since Jonathan's departure Mina had spent much of her time worrying about her fiancé, far off in Eastern Europe, though she kept trying to tell herself that her worries were unreasonable. It did not help that more than a week had passed and she had received no communication from Jonathan except one brief letter, posted in Paris, and containing no real news.

Lucy, in her new party dress, now came hurrying along the upstairs hall. "There you are! Mina, come on down. Someone simply has to help me entertain them all tonight. Mother enjoys parties as a rule, but she's not really up to them any longer."

Mina said distantly: "I'll be down in a moment. . . ."

"Oh, come! It will be good for you, distract you from your worries about Jonathan."

Catching her reflection in a wall mirror, Lucy primped at her red hair. "I'm so happy I don't know what to do with myself! I think I'm about to have three marriage proposals in one evening. Oh, Mina, I hope there is enough of me to share!"

That was enough to distract Mina despite herself. "You certainly can't marry all three!"

"Why not?" Lucy turned to her friend. Her question seemed almost serious; certainly it sounded like a plea for help. "Tell me, *why* can't a girl marry three men, or as many as want her?"

Mina was saved from having to attempt an explanation when Lucy was distracted by the latest arrival in the hall below. She whispered excitedly: "Here comes one of my three now!"

The newest guest at the party presented a striking figure indeed, that of a tall, dark-mustached young man wearing a wide-brimmed hat and boots belonging to the American west. All of his clothing looked expensive, but by London standards definitely unconventional. Occasionally visible under the skirt of his coat at his left side was a long leather sheath evidently depending from his belt.

Mina was fascinated despite herself. "What is that?"

Lucy said proudly: "*That* is a Texan. Quincey P. Morris. A friend of Arthur's, and also of Dr. Seward. The three of them have been adventuring all over the world."

"And Mr. Morris has proposed to you?"

"Well—I expect him to do so at any moment. Isn't it wonderful, Mina? He's so young and fresh. I can imagine him as—as a wild stallion, between my legs."

Mina blushed, and at the same time had to stifle an improper laugh. "You are positively indecent!"

"I know—don't worry, dear, I only say those things to make you blush; you do it so prettily."

"I really hope that is the only reason you say them. And what is that sheathed object Mr. Morris carries under his coat?"

Lucy struggled with her own laughter. "Dear Quincey carries with him everywhere a very impressive—tool!"

"Lucy!"

"But he does, dear—he truly does. I'll show you!" And Lucy went skipping down the stair, only adopting a somewhat more sedate pace when she reached the floor below and moved to welcome Quincey.

Mina watched from upstairs as Lucy took his arm, freely sidling up to the tall man in a way that brought a frosty glance of disapproval from her mother on the other side of the great hall.

A moment later Lucy had actually reached under the Texan's coat and drawn an enormous bowie knife from its sheath, waving the footlong blade gaily in the direction of Mina, who was just beginning to descend the stairs.

For half an hour Mina mingled dutifully with other guests. Then she again drifted to the fringe of the party. She was momentarily alone with her thoughts, struggling with her worries concerning Jonathan, when Lucy once more approached her.

This time the red-haired girl was quietly ecstatic. "They're *all* here. I *do* think I'm about to have three marriage proposals in one day. What shall I do?"

Mina scarcely knew whether to laugh or to worry seriously about her friend's romantic difficulties. "Then the Texan has proposed?"

"Yes!"

Mina looked for Mr. Quincey Morris and discovered him on the other side of the room, gazing soulfully in Lucy's direction. "I am almost afraid to ask *what?*"

"Marriage!" Lucy, concentrating entirely on her own feelings, was oblivious to the dry humor in Mina's question.

She gave the impression of hanging balanced between joy and panic. "I told him there's another. . . . I did not say two others, but actually they're all going to be here—look, that's Dr. Jack Seward coming in now."

At the far end of the great hall an intense-looking man in his early thirties was just giving his hat and gloves into the custody of a servant.

"He's brilliant," Lucy went on. "Still young enough to be interesting, but already has an immense lunatic asylum all under his own care. I thought he would just do for you, if you were not already engaged."

"Lunatics! I see. And so naturally you thought of me."

There was a touch of cruelty in Lucy's laughter. Then her face, as she gazed past Mina's shoulder, took on an expression Mina had not seen her wear before.

Turning, Mina beheld a man she had heard of but not yet met

entering the hall. A guest who could only be the Honorable Arthur Holmwood, the future Lord Godalming, had arrived close on the heels of Dr. Seward. Holmwood, wealthy, handsome, and imperious, was exchanging uneasy looks with the doctor.

"Number three?" Mina inquired softly.

She received no verbal reply, but there was really no need for one. The answer was plain in Lucy's face, and reflected in the joy demonstrated in turn by the latest arrival, as she hurried across the crowded floor to meet him.

On that same night, in the remote Carpathians, the young solicitor Jonathan Harker was entering the library of Castle Dracula. There he found the count lying on the sofa, reading ("of all things," as Harker later commented in his journal) an English Bradshaw's guide, a compendium of schedules for the railway system and other means of transportation.

Harker stopped in his tracks upon thus encountering his host. But the count, his manner as cheerful and pleasant as if there had never been any such difficulties as mirrors and razors between them, sat up and greeted his young guest in a hearty way.

"I am glad you found your way in here, for I am sure there is much that will interest you. These friends"—and here Dracula laid his long-nailed hand on some of the books—"have been good friends to me, and for some years past have given me many, many hours of pleasure. Through them I have come to know your great England; and to know her is to love her. But alas, as yet I know your tongue only through books. To you, my friend, I look that I know it to speak."

"But, Count," Harker assured him, "you know and speak English thoroughly!"

Dracula, still sitting on the sofa, nodded gravely. "I thank you, my friend, for your all-too-flattering estimate, but yet I fear I am but a little way on the road I would travel. True, I know the grammar and the words, but yet I know not how to speak them."

"Indeed," the young Englishman persisted, "you speak excellently."

"Not so," the old man answered. "Well I know that did I move and speak in your London, none there are among your countrymen who would not know me for a stranger. That is not enough for me. Here I am noble; I am *boyar;* the common people know me, and I am master. But a stranger in a strange land, he is no one; men know him not—and to know not is to care not for.

"I have been so long master that I would be master still—or at least that none other should be master of me."

Harker could only agree with this view, which he considered quite reasonable; and for some time the conversation proceeded, as between two rational and intelligent men, touching on many subjects.

Only when the young man raised the subject of his possible departure from the castle was he brusquely dismissed.

The days passed for Harker largely in slumber, and the nights in reading or wandering, or long rambling conversations with the count. To Harker time seemed to perish, in a kind of eerie monotony of existence, until he could no longer feel absolutely certain of the dates he wrote down in his journal.

The hardest thing to bear was his concern for Mina—the pride she had felt in his achievement must long ago have turned to worry, and then to fear—not only for his safety, but that the lack of any word from him might mean his love had cooled, even that he had been unfaithful.

Eventually a night came when the young man left his rooms determined to dare a bolder exploration of the castle than any he had yet attempted in his weeks of involuntary confinement.

Gradually he had become convinced that his condition in this place could only be described as confinement. As his time as an increasingly unwilling guest had lengthened into weeks, his methodical explorations, first tentative, then carried on with increasing urgency, had brought him to a dread discovery; there were doors, doors, doors everywhere, but almost all of them the doors of a fortress, locked and bolted! In no place save from the high windows was there an available exit.

The castle was a veritable prison, and he was indeed a prisoner!

When Harker reached that conclusion, a wild feeling came over him; he rushed up and down stairs, trying every door and peering out of every window he could find. But the conviction of helplessness soon overpowered all other feelings.

At that point he sat down quietly—as quietly as he had ever done anything in his life—and began to think.

Of one thing only was he immediately certain—that it was no use making his ideas or fears on the subject known to the count. If he, Harker, was indeed a prisoner, the count was well aware of the fact, being himself responsible.

This night, having as he thought already explored every available downward path that might logically have led him to some opportunity for escape, Harker tried a new tactic and went up. An ascending stone stair he had not tried before brought him to a vantage point from which he could look out of the castle toward the south, over miles of the surrounding countryside. Straight below him lay nothing but a terrible precipice, of castle wall atop sheer cliff, and at last a river, perhaps a thousand feet below. There was some sense of freedom in the vast expanse, inaccessible though it was, as compared with the narrow darkness of the courtyard, all that was visible from the windows of his apartment.

Rejoicing in the momentary sense of freedom, he gazed out over the beautiful countryside, bathed in soft yellow moonlight, so that there was an illusion of almost daylight visibility. In the soft radiance the distant hills became melted, and the shadows in the valleys and gorges were of velvety blackness.

Here, Harker, despite the increasing certainty that he was indeed a captive, found a measure of peace and comfort in every breath he drew. But presently, as the young Englishman leaned from the window, his eye was caught by some object moving on the castle wall a level below him and somewhat to his left. It was there he imagined, from what he knew of the interior order of the rooms, that the windows of the count's own chamber must probably lie.

The window at which Harker had found his observation post was tall and deep. He drew back behind the stonework at its side and looked out carefully.

In a moment Harker saw the count's head emerging from the lower window. He did not see the face, but, even at a little distance and by moonlight, knew the man by the neck and the movement of his back and arms. In any case, Harker thought, he could not ever possibly mistake those hands.

Harker's feelings of curiosity changed to repulsion and terror when he observed the whole man slowly emerge from the window and begin to crawl down the castle wall over that dreadful abyss, *facedown*, with his cloak spreading out around him like great wings. At first the young man watching could not believe his eyes. He thought what he was seeing must be some trick of the moonlight, some weird effect of shadow. But soon he was forced to admit his conviction that it could be no delusion.

What manner of man was this, or what manner of creature in the semblance of a man?

Harker recoiled from the window, feeling the dread of the horrible place overpowering him; he was in fear—in awful fear—and there was no escape. . . .

Gradually Harker managed to control his nerves. Feeling at least assured that the count had left the castle for the time being, he nerved himself for a bolder attempt at exploration.

He went quickly back to his rooms and, taking a fresh lamp, from there down the stone stairs to the hall where he had entered the castle originally. He found he could pull back the bolts of the front door easily enough and, with some effort, unhook the great chains; but still the door was locked and the key was gone.

There were no tools at hand with which he might hope to attack the formidable barrier successfully; and, as usual, he could hear the wolves howling at no very great distance beyond it. He feared he would not long survive the opening of this door tonight.

But he was not going to give up. From the great hall he went on to make a more methodical examination than before of all the various stairs and passages to which he had access, and to try the doors that opened from them. One or two small rooms near the hall were open, but there was nothing to see in them except old furniture.

At last he found one door, near the top of the highest accessible stairway, which he had not yet tried to open. Though this door seemed at first to be locked, when Harker leaned his weight against the surface, it yielded a little under pressure.

The young man put his shoulder to the old wood and tried again. It gave a little more.

When Harker strained his muscles to the limit, the barrier suddenly gave way—the door had not been locked, but only stuck—and he fell into the room beyond.

Slowly, brushing dust from hands and knees, he got to his feet. It was almost as if he had entered a new world entirely. Picking up his lamp from where he had set it down, he advanced slowly, holding the lamp high, moving through room after room.

Here, high, broad windows, protected by the sheer precipice below from any danger of enemy attack, admitted a flood of moonlight. This, Harker decided, must have been the portion of the castle that had been occupied by the ladies in bygone centuries. Somehow the furniture—and there was quite a bit of it—had more air of comfort. He thought a feminine touch was clearly detectable in the arrangement and the decoration.

The big windows were completely free of any drape or curtain, and the yellow moonlight, flooding in through diamond panes, enabled one to see even colors. . . . The intruder's lamp, which he now raised again, seemed to be of little effect in the brilliant, silent moonlight.

Slight, swift motion at the corner of his eye caught Harker's attention—it was that of a long-legged spider scampering across the top of an old and beautiful vanity or dressing table, its mirror draped with what appeared to be a silken cloth.

The top of the antique dressing table was almost crowded with bottles and combs, brushes and powders. Harker stood beside it, touching one item after another on its top. He noticed that his fingers trembled. Yes, women had lived here. . . . Almost it appeared to the intruder that they still did.

One perfume bottle in particular appeared so fragile and lovely in the half-magical illumination that Harker felt compelled to touch it again to make sure that it was real. Gently he lifted the small container from the dust in which it rested. Without thought his fingers found and pulled out the stopper, releasing a faint drop of delicious scent, which he could not identify, but which made his senses tingle. He thought he saw the droplet clearly for a moment, but then it seemed to vanish immediately into the air.

The air itself felt like it was pulsating around him. He put the perfume bottle down again.

Moving now with the feeling of having entered a dream, he turned away from the small table, to find himself confronted by silken hangings and piles of many pillows. What he had thought at first sight might be a divan was actually a large bed, which spread itself invitingly before him.

Dully Harker noticed, without giving the fact much thought, that his lamp had gone out, and he put it on the floor. His legs were suddenly very tired, and he sat down upon the edge of the bed to rest. Again a wave—not of dust, but of perfume—as before impossible to identify but delicious, entrancing, rose about him, even more subtly than before.

Truly, his arms and legs were weakened with fatigue, with the long strain of fear. Here in this chamber, on this bed, it seemed possible that fear could be forgotten. If only he could rest . . . the silks of the soft bed invited him to recline. They seemed to undulate, to fit themselves beneath his body and around it.

In the dreamlike state he had now entered, it came as no shock to Harker to discover that he was no longer alone. The beautiful tenants of these women's quarters were with him now—and it seemed he had known for a long time that they must be.

Three of them, all young, all ladies by their dress and manner, though two were dark as Gypsies, with great dark piercing eyes that seemed almost red when contrasted with the pale yellow moon—he noted with interest, but with no terror as yet, that snakes moved in the hair of one. All three women had brilliant white teeth that shone like pearls against the ruby of their voluptuous lips.

The third, the youngest as Harker supposed her to be, was fair as fair can be, with great wavy masses of golden hair, and eyes like pale sapphires.

And it seemed to the young man who was now lying on her bed—he knew it must be hers—that he had somehow in the past known this blond girl's face, in connection with some dreamy fear, but at the moment he could not recollect how or where the meeting had occurred.

Though the moonlight fell from behind the women, their bodies seemed to throw no shadows on the floor. And now Harker could see quite plainly that the three of them were wearing very little more than moonlight, only moonlight and the faintest gossamer. . . . The three whispered together, and then they laughed—such a silvery, musical laugh, but hard, as hard as metal, as though the sound never could have come through the softness of human lips. It struck the man's ears like the intolerable, tingling sweetness of music made on the rims of wineglasses, played by a cunning hand.

The fair girl, looking straight at Harker now, shook her head coquettishly, and the others seemed to urge her on.

The voice of one of the dark women, she who seemed somehow

a little older than the others, had the same quality of sound as their sweet laughter.

"Go on!" she urged the youngest. "You are first, and we shall follow."

The younger brunette added her incitement: "He is young and strong, there will be kisses for us all."

It seemed to Harker that it was quite impossible for him to move—it would be hopeless even to attempt the effort. He decided this, with satisfaction, as the fair girl, moving in utter and unnatural silence, came closer to him and knelt beside the couch. Then she bent over him until it seemed that he could smell and taste the unbearable sweetness of her breath, like honey with something quite different under it, the bitterness of the smell of blood.

Suddenly sharp fingernails were on his chest, his arms, his legs, biting his skin like insects, slitting his clothing like steel knives, catching in the fabric and peeling it away. He could do nothing, and he wanted to do nothing.

The blond girl arched her neck and licked her lips, and in the moonlight he could see her body, all of it, the last gossamer covering now gone, and the moisture shining on the scarlet lips and on the red tongue as it lapped the sharp white teeth.

The blond hair came billowing over Harker's face like a cloud of perfume as the girl bent down. He was aware now that sharp teeth were biting at the cord of his small silver crucifix—let the cross go, he thought, and there it went. And now the other women, too impatient after all to wait their turns, had come to join him on the bed, and their bodies pressed upon him, and their dark hair, snakes and all, was trailing everywhere over his exposed flesh. And still he could not move. Could not. And at the same time he was afraid even to breathe, to stir a finger, lest they should cease what they were doing. And now he could feel their lips, three pairs of lips, three tongues.

And now their teeth, so exquisitely sharp.

So sweet . . .

Out of nowhere, as it seemed, interruption came.

Somewhere nearby, very close at hand, the storm of fury was rushing on. . . .

Harker groaned with a sharp sense of loss. Insupportable deprivation. His eyes snapped open involuntarily, just in time to see the count's white hand, inhumanly hairy on the palm and inhumanly strong, clamp itself onto the slender neck of the fair woman.

The young man caught only a brief glimpse of her furious blue eyes before Dracula, with a fierce sweep of his arm, hurled her away across the room. Threw her bodily, as if she had been only a child, a doll.

"How dare you touch him?" The master's voice was low, but the anger and the danger in it might have crumbled stone. "How dare you, when I have forbidden it? This man belongs to me!"

The youngest, lying in the moonlight where he had thrown her, lying in an awkward, almost insectlike pose, raised a face transformed with fury. "To you? You never loved. *You never love!*"

The other two women had distanced themselves from Harker now, and it seemed to him that all of them were clothed again. Still he lay in the exact position where they had left him. He felt himself possessed by a languorous, unnatural lethargy, and wondered if he might be dreaming. Again his eyes closed, without his willing it.

When Harker slitted open his lids and looked again, the three women had all crept close, submissively, to Dracula.

In a different voice, more controlled, the count was saying to them: "Yes—I, too, can love. You yourselves can tell it from the past—you have all been my brides—and I shall love again."

He gestured contemptuously in Harker's general direction. "I promise you, when I have done with him—it is a matter of business—then you shall kiss him at your will."

The youngest of his brides was pouting, sulking. "Are we to have nothing tonight?"

Silently, the tall, dark figure of their master pulled out a bag from under his cloak and cast it on the floor. There came to Harker's ears a gasp and a low wail, as of a half-smothered child; and with that sound, horror overcame him utterly, and he knew no more.

6

ven now, weeks after the fact, Dr. Jack Seward's thoughts were still more than half-occupied with the bitter knowledge that Lucy Westenra had refused to marry him.

It hardly helped to know that she had also turned down Quincey Morris, the wealthy Texan who had been Seward's frequent companion in big-game hunting, or that Quincey was also hard hit by his rejection. In Dr. Seward's case, his work, challenging intellectual work, seemed the only effective and honorable remedy for his bruised pride; and at least in the asylum there was work aplenty for the physician.

The asylum of which bright, still-youthful Dr. Seward had been given the superintendency was an old building in suburban London. It stood comfortably secluded amid its own extensive, wooded, walled-in grounds, as was only fitting for an establishment catering almost exclusively to a wealthy clientele. Once it had been a mansion, like Carfax, the long-deserted house on one of the adjoining estates. The asylum was old, though by all accounts not nearly so old as Carfax; and it had been recently remodeled, largely at Seward's direction, into the architectural configuration required for a more or less efficient and humane hospital, meeting the latest medical standards of these last years of the nineteenth century.

At the moment Dr. Seward was halfway through his evening rounds. Around him, from behind one barred door after another, arose, as usual, the outraged and incoherent cries of the insane. Seward was accustomed to them, and heard them with only half an ear.

Lucy, Lucy! Not only was the young girl lovely, physically provocative enough to threaten a suitor's mental health, but since she was the heiress to Hillingham as well, it was definitely understating the case to say that she was well-to-do.

When Lucy's mother died—an event which, given the parlous state of the old lady's heart, lay probably not very far in the future—Lucy ought to be in line to inherit . . .

But enough of that. The fact remained that Lucy Westenra had rejected him, a handsome and prosperous physician, rapidly making his way toward the top of his profession. She had tendered her refusal with a flattering suggestion of reluctance, but still very definitely. And who could blame her, when she had the chance to marry, in the person of Art Holmwood, a future earl?

Jack Seward had come to realize over the past few weeks that it was not really Lucy Westenra's money or even her tantalizing body that he was going to miss the most. The hardest part, it seemed, was that he genuinely loved the girl. . . .

Now the door of yet another cell clattered open, unlocked by the hands of an attendant. Seward's professional interest quickened, temporarily driving even thoughts of Lucy from his mind. He had been looking forward to visiting this particular patient. Here, now, was a real oddity.

The single window of the small stone cell, like most of the windows in the house, was coarsely barred to prevent human escape—or intrusion. But this window was currently open to the outside air, even to the passage of sparrows and other birds. That some of these small winged creatures were frequently lured in was attested to by the fact that the floor was encrusted with bird droppings. In the corners of the cell substantial quantities of food intended for the patient's nourishment had been deliberately crumbled and smeared, allowed to decay, in order to attract a multitude of flies.

The two attendants who tonight were accompanying Dr. Seward on his rounds—both of them powerfully built men—stopped and waited just outside the cell. Seward himself stepped just inside the door, repressing an urge to gag at the smell. Perhaps in this case his favored policy of toleration for a patient's eccentricity had been a mistake after all.

He said: "Good evening, Mr. Renfield."

The cell's sole human occupant looked up. He was a balding, sturdy man of middle age, dressed in the coarse shirt and trousers usually issued to male patients. His person, in contrast to his cell, was neat and clean. He was wearing thick-lensed eyeglasses and, at the moment, a pleasant expression. Turning to Dr. Seward, Renfield revealed that he was holding in his right hand a plate of insects, worms, and spiders. Seward had the impression that all the creatures were alive but somehow immobilized.

"Hors d'oeuvres, Dr. Seward? Canapés?" The voice was cultured, the manner calm.

"No, thank you, Mr. Renfield. How are you feeling tonight?"

"Far better than you, my lovesick doctor." And the madman casually turned his back upon his visitor.

Carefully setting down his plate and its precious contents, Renfield squatted in a corner and deftly went about catching some of the many flies that swarmed about his bait of decomposing food heavily sprinkled with sugar. His strong, thick-fingered hands were quick and accurate at this task. Flies buzzed in protest as he carefully gathered them, alive, into one of his capable fists.

Lovesick. Well, of course attendants and servants would often gossip in front of the patients. Seward, so far on this visit, was managing to keep his own reactions scientifically neutral.

"Is my personal life of interest to you?" he inquired.

"All life interests me," Renfield responded as he went blandly on with his self-appointed task.

Then, with a gesture as of one about to drink a toast, he brought his handful of flies to his mouth. Only one or two escaped as he popped them in. With evident relish he chewed and swallowed.

Tonight Seward was finding the scientific attitude very difficult to maintain. "Your diet, Mr. Renfield, is disgusting."

The eyes of the former solicitor twinkled behind his glasses, as if to acknowledge a compliment. "Perfectly nutritious. Each life I ingest gives back life to me, augments my own vitality."

He held up one more fly, large, blue black, and juicy looking, between thumb and forefinger for a moment. Then it went to join the previous handful.

Seward was struggling to maintain some objectivity. "A fly gives you life?"

As Seward had hoped, the patient tonight was willing, even eager, to discuss his theory. "The fly's sapphire wings are typical of the aerial powers of the psychic faculties. Therefore the ancients did well when they typified the soul of a man as a butterfly!"

"Is this some philosophic insight that you gained during your recent visit to Eastern Europe?"

No reply.

"I think"—Seward sighed—"I shall have to invent a new classification of lunatic for you."

"Really? Perhaps you can improve upon the classification devised by your old mentor, Professor Van Helsing: *zoophagous arachnophile*—a carnivorous lover of spiders. Of course that does not really, fully, describe my case."

With a deft movement Renfield bent over the plate he had set down, caught up one of the spiders from it, considered the creature momentarily, and ate it.

"Yes, what about the spiders?" Seward was musing aloud, more to himself than to Renfield or the husky, impassive keepers who continued to stand by just outside the cell. "How do spiders fit into your theory? I suppose they eat the flies. . . ."

"Oh, yes, spiders eat them." Renfield's manner suddenly became that of a teacher coaxing a bright student toward an answer. He nodded at Seward encouragingly.

The doctor was beginning to catch on—or so he thought. "And the sparrows?"

"Yes, the sparrows!" Now the patient's excitement was growing rapidly.

"They eat the spiders, I presume."

"Yes, yes!"

Seward nodded. "Thus we would come, by a logical progression, to . . . something . . . even larger, perhaps? Some creature capable of devouring sparrows?"

Renfield, his agitation suddenly building toward frenzy, threw himself on his knees on the stone floor.

He cried out, beseeching Seward in seeming desperation: "A kitten! A nice, little, sleek, playful kitten, that I can teach and feed and feed. No one would refuse a kitten—I implore you—"

The doctor, his eyes narrowed, took a step backward to be free of the man's clutching hands. He could hear the pair of keepers behind him shifting their positions, ready to intervene if necessary.

Leaning toward Renfield, Seward spoke with calculation. "Wouldn't you rather have a cat?"

Ecstasy! *"Yes, yes, a cat!"* Screaming! "A big cat. *My salvation depends upon it!"*

"Your salvation?"

Renfield's expression, his whole manner, altered. Something like calm returned.

Regaining his feet, the patient looked Seward straight in the eye. "Lives," he said simply. "It all comes down to that. I need lives for the Master."

The doctor blinked. This was new. "What 'master'? Do you mean Professor Van Helsing?"

The lunatic's scorn and contempt were enormous. "No! The *Master!* He will come."

"Here? To the asylum?"

"Yes!"

"Here to your cell?"

"*Yes!*"

"Why?"

"He has promised to make me immortal!"

"How?"

Somehow this simple question was the one that probed too close to the nerve. With a strangled cry Renfield lurched forward, his powerful hands groping for a grip. The pair of attendants in the corridor had not relaxed their vigilance, and they rushed in at once to interfere; still they were a shade too late, and both of the madman's fists were clamped on Seward's collar. Renfield's jaws that had chewed flies and spiders were now ravening for a bite at Seward's throat.

Gasps and curses. Three men against one, in a swaying struggle. Other patients in other cells, aware of violence in progress, set up an eerie clamoring.

Seward, far from a weakling himself, was gripping Renfield's wrists with all his strength, trying to tear the choking hands away—but to no avail. The madman's arms seemed carved from stone. Seward's lungs were bursting, and the world was turning red and gray before the doctor's eyes.

Renfield was screaming maniacally now: "The blood is the life. *The blood is the life!*"

One of the keepers had the patient around the neck from behind, keeping him from biting; the other had him by a shoulder and an arm. But even with odds of three to one, mere wrestling was not going to save Dr. Seward from being throttled. Now clubs rose and fell. But still, one keeper had a broken arm before the lunatic was finally subdued.

7

It was morning again in the Carpathians, gray early daylight on a day of spring rain that came spattering and lashing intermittently at the high windows of the apartment which had become Harker's refuge, overlooking the still-deserted courtyard of Dracula's castle.

Harker had awakened in his usual room within the castle, in his usual bed, and for one blessed moment before his eyelids opened he had been able to persuade himself that his experience with the three women had been only a dream.

For one moment only—then, despite all the improbability and nightmarish horror of what had happened, he was soon utterly convinced that their embraces had been as real as any other experience he had ever had.

His shredded clothing testified to the reality of that particular nightmare, as did certain painless, seemingly harmless, but terrifying marks—suggesting the action of fine, sharp teeth—in at least three places on his body. His private parts, his very manhood, had not been spared.

To have yielded to temptation with a woman, or women, in the normal way would have been bad enough for an engaged man. Especially, as it seemed to Harker, for any man whom Mina loved. But *this* . . . !

Overcome by shame, by the helpless certainty of unnatural guilt, Harker sat for some time on the edge of his bed, face buried in his hands. He was struggling not only with his guilt, but against the memory of great delight.

At length, pulling himself together, he made a new resolve to face his difficulties, however great they might be, and overcome them. From now on he must, he would, maintain his self-respect, live in a manner worthy of the great love that Mina bore him in her innocence.

It must have been the count himself, he decided at length, who had carried him back to bed in this room and undressed him. A number of small details, even apart from the torn clothing and the wounds, testified that Harker's nightly routine had not gone as usual; his pocket watch, for one thing, was unwound, and he was rigorously accustomed to wind it before retiring. But the contents of his pockets, in particular his journal, seemed undisturbed—for which he breathed a small prayer of thankfulness. He felt sure that if Dracula had noticed the small book, he would have stolen or destroyed it. Perhaps the count for some reason had been hurried in his task.

Slowly Harker bathed—once deprived of his mirror, he had abandoned all attempts to shave—and dressed himself in untorn garments from his trunk. He was perfectly certain, long before he looked, that this morning as usual there would be a breakfast laid out for him in the next room, decent food on golden plates or perhaps on silver, even coffee warming on the hearth. Evidently his usefulness, as language teacher and adviser on the ways of England, was not yet over.

But today he was not hungry.

For some time after getting dressed, he occupied the chair at the writing desk in his sitting room, making an entry in his journal. Harker considered this record a necessary part of his determined effort to keep a grip upon his sanity. He even noted down, as clearly and objectively as possible, despite the chance that Mina might someday read his words, what he remembered of his experience with the three women.

Then, startled by hearing unaccustomed noises outside in the courtyard—raucous human shouts and the rumble of wagons—he hastily replaced the small volume in an inner pocket of his coat and went to the window to look out.

To his amazement Harker saw that the place was deserted no longer. As he watched he observed that a sizable work party composed of Gypsies, the Szgany as Harker had learned they were called in this country, was undertaking a considerable task, that of loading great coffin-sized boxes, obviously heavy, aboard several sturdy leiter wagons, the wagons hitched to teams of four to six horses each. There were three boxes, four—another and another. Soon Harker realized, from the number of wagons, that there might be dozens of these containers, all the same size and shape, each emblazoned with Dracula's coat of arms. They were being carried out, one by one, into the open courtyard from somewhere inside the castle. The location of Harker's window kept him from seeing exactly where the source might be.

The Szgany were going cheerfully and noisily about their task of loading the strange cargo. Shortly after discovering their presence, Harker took a position in full view in his window, quietly trying to signal to some of the men below. His hope was to get one of them to post a truthful letter to England, a message that would alert his employer to the fact that he was being held here as a prisoner. But only a few workers took any notice of the man in the window, and these only jeered at him, even ignoring the coins he held up in an effort to arouse their interest.

After that, trembling with fear and anger, he lurked near the window, continuing to observe the unaccustomed activity in the courtyard, as much as possible without being observed himself.

The visible boxes multiplied; as soon as a wagon was fully loaded, it was driven away and out, and an empty vehicle pulled up to take its place. When one of the large boxes slipped just as it was being hoisted aboard a wagon and broke open with the force of its impact on the stone paving, Harker saw moldy, greenish, foul-looking earth spill out, ugly stuff that at once began to turn to mud in the persistent drizzle.

The accident had a sobering effect upon the laborers. Their merry songs and laughter ceased abruptly, and they cast frequent glances over their shoulders, and up at the high windows of the castle. Clearly they dreaded their employer's wrath. Not only the Szgany but even the horses, as it seemed to Harker, were frightened at the spillage. The men made haste to repair the damage, finding somewhere fresh boards with which to rebuild the box, replaced the contents as thoroughly as they could, and got on with their work.

Shortly after that Harker drew back from the window. That a shipment of moldy earth was being made from Castle Dracula was puzzling, but there were more urgent problems to be faced.

Obviously he dared hope for no help from the Gypsies, who were laboring faithfully on their mysterious task for the castle's master. Therefore, as it seemed to him, he had two choices. First, he could wait in his rooms, or visit the library again, or employ himself in other useless ways, until cloudy daylight should give way to night.

Then, when night had fallen, the three women—Harker was as sure of it as if they had promised him in so many words—would come to his door. Now that they had established a relationship with him, they would inevitably come, to laugh and whisper just outside, promising renewed delight, tempting him unbearably, until he should yield and come out to them . . . and he knew that he would yield.

But his blood chilled at the thought that perhaps the women had indeed given him just such a promise, or such a warning, last night while he lay in that helpless trance.

Harker shuddered violently at the compound memory of horror and pain and pleasure. But no, *they* were not women—Mina was a woman. Those three were devils of the pit!

Whenever he closed his eyes, he could see again the movement of that bag the count had thrown before them, and could hear again the half-stifled human cry that came from it. Whether in true memory, or only in imagination, he could see the naked babe drawn forth from it by the white, long-nailed hand. . . .

But now, in daylight, he, the prisoner, still had time to make one other choice. He could summon up the courage of his growing despair and attempt an escape, by taking the only open path, the one he had once seen used by Dracula himself.

Harker could attempt to get away by climbing down the castle wall.

Thinking coldly and clearly now, the young man could accept that choice, though it was hideously dangerous, in fact almost suicidal. He preferred death at the bottom of the cliffs to whatever fate the count and the three horrible, fascinating women might have in store for him.

If he was ever going to attempt the castle wall, obviously the effort must be made by day. And evidently it would be hopeless to try to escape on the side of the castle where Dracula's loyal servants the Gypsies could observe him.

Therefore he must go on the other side, the side above the dreadful cliff. And he must leave his rooms to do it now—now, at once—before fear—and the terrible attraction of what awaited him tonight—could combine to undo his resolve.

Plainly he would be able to carry with him nothing but what

might fit in his pockets—his journal, some money, and very little else.

Leaving his rooms on impulse, not allowing himself a chance to hesitate, Harker once more mounted the high stair that led to the south side of the castle, to the windows that overlooked the steepest precipice, and the twisting, leaping river that foamed below, too far below for him to hear the water's roar.

Misty rain blew in his face. He was standing at the same window where he had hidden and watched with horror as the count himself climbed down the wall.

Now Harker, gripping the wet stone of the sill so that the muscles trembled in his arms, allowed himself to look down, all the way down, once.

The terror of the sight was not as great as he had feared.

In fact the outer surface of the castle wall beneath him now was very nearly sheer, but not so absolutely featureless as to make his attempt completely suicidal. A very slight general inward slope from bottom to top, combined with the roughness of the stones, and the many seams and broken, crumbling edges, offered at least faint hope that the fingers and toes of an ordinary human might be able to find enough purchase for the climb. The first forty or fifty feet, he thought, would be the worst—below that the irregularities grew greater, and there would be real hope.

Gritting his teeth, the young man whispered: "If I should find *him* on my way, I must kill him. Good-bye, Mina, if I fail. Good-bye, all!"

Muttering a prayer, still not allowing himself time to hesitate, Harker went over the rain-wet sill and out, lowering himself on nerve and will and fingertips.

But these, his only real assets, quickly proved inadequate. Harker had descended only a few feet along his dreadful path before the grip of his fingers upon the ancient stonework abruptly failed.

A hoarse cry of despair burst from his throat.

Slipping and sliding down an almost vertical incline, bloodying his hands in a desperate effort to stop his fall, Harker came to an abrupt and unexpected halt, crashing into the muck and water that filled most of a stone basin or huge gargoylish cup built out from the castle's flank.

Spitting and choking on foul water, he brought his face above the surface. Dimly he realized that this tub-sized receptacle might once have been part of a system of cisterns for gathering rainwater.

Shuddering now with the realization of how close he had come to sudden death, Harker looked about him from this precarious place of momentary safety. To right and left there was no chance, only blank vertical stone for many yards. Below, the hopeless wall fell straight away to nothing more secure than a dizzying plunge of equally hopeless rock, ending only in the river at its unreal distance.

But now a faint new possibility had presented itself. From the stone basin in which Harker crouched, a low, dark tunnel of a drain, barely wide enough to accommodate a man's body, led back—somewhere—into the castle wall. The drain was mostly clogged, with broken stones and mud, but he could dig the obstacles away. As he did so, the water that had saved his life went gurgling off.

There was no real alternative. Breathing another prayer, the young man crawled headfirst into the tunnel.

Through many tight spots and sharp turns this passage led him along a wearying, seemingly endless descent. Through gaps in crumbling, broken masonry, through darkness and foul smells, by means of many, many reversals and windings, he went down. Spiderwebs brushed at his face. Rats and other things went scurrying away from him; the hardness and roughness of stone wore at his knees and elbows, through the wet fabric of coat and trousers.

Down, always down.

A time came when Harker felt he had descended for such a distance that he must now be at least close to the level of the courtyard. He thought that it might well be fatal to emerge among the jeering Szgany, who had given every evidence of being the faithful servants of his mortal enemy.

Go slowly now! Be quiet!

Very cautiously, now making a conscious effort to cause as little noise as possible, he crawled on.

At last providence, or fortune, or some benign power, seemed to smile on him. Harker managed to avoid encountering the Gypsies when he at last crawled out of the castle's wall through a great fracture in its thickness. Instead of being in the familiar courtyard, he found himself in an extensive chamber, whose darkness was so much modified by indirect sunlight that the heart of the fugitive rose in hope, thinking that the blessed outdoors and the possibility of freedom must be very near.

Careful, though! Standing erect again, nursing his bloodied knees and elbows, he could clearly hear the Szgany singing their work songs. But their voices sounded from sufficiently far away to present, as he thought, no immediate danger.

Stretching limbs cramped by the long, tortuous, crawling descent, peering cautiously about him, Harker soon understood that this dim chamber to which chance had brought him must be—rather, must once have been—a chapel. He thought the place looked very old, from the fifteenth century or even earlier.

Large sections of the walls were honeycombed with what Harker quickly realized must be burial vaults, aboveground sepulchers; and in front of a tall window whose antique glass was still intact, a simple altar (he could read the word DRACULEA carved across the front) supported a great wooden cross.

The carven front of this tall symbol was all stained as by dried blood. For some reason, as Harker gazed at this forsaken cross, his eyes began to fill with tears, and he felt at his throat for the small silver crucifix that was no longer there.

Parts of the floor of this dim, cavernous room had long ago been broken up, so that the dark and almost lifeless earth beneath bulged through. Someone had recently been digging in this exposed earth—there were modern shovels, and a spade.

And all across this broken floor, arranged in rows, were more of the strange, coffinlike wooden boxes, evidently waiting to be loaded on the wagons. One box, with its lid in place like the others, but not yet nailed down as the others seemed to be, rested by itself at a little distance from them.

Now somewhere near at hand, no more than a few yards away, Harker could hear the Gypsies once more shouting to each other as they nailed and lifted and loaded. He heard the clatter of wagon wheels on cobblestones, the snap of whips.

As the fugitive looked about him, seeking the best chance of completing his escape, his eye was caught by a faint, strange gleam in the indirect daylight. Something yellow, just there where soil showed through the broken pavement. Moving in cautious silence to the spot, Harker bent to pick up first one gold coin of old and unfamiliar mintage, then another. Quickly, with the idea that it might be of use to him in his escape, he was able to gather a small handful of treasure that had been lying here mixed into the ground.

Almost too late he became aware that the voices of the Szgany had suddenly grown louder. Hastily the intruder sprang up and pressed himself back into a recess of the wall. A moment later several Gypsies came in through the main entrance of the chapel, to lift and bear out with them, grunting, one more of the coffins.

As soon as they were gone again Harker emerged from hiding. For the moment the need for knowledge was even stronger than the urge to escape.

Approaching the coffin that stood a little apart from the others, Harker seized and wrenched off the lid, which was still unfastened. Gazing at the revealed contents, he froze in fright and horror.

Dracula, garbed in an ornate robe of golden and bejeweled fabric, was looking back at him.

It took Harker a long, nightmarish moment to realize that the eyes of the man in the box, though they were turned in his direction, did not see him, or at any rate were not really focused upon him.

No doubt, though, that it was the count himself who lay faceup inside the coffin of the dark mold, as an ordinary man might recline upon some soft and pleasant bed.

Recovering moment by moment, breath by breath, from the initial shock of the discovery, Harker realized that Dracula must be either dead or asleep—he felt unable to say which, for the count's open eyes were without either the alertness of life or the glassiness of death. The cheeks seemed to retain the warmth of life through all their pallor; the lips were red, and bore stains of what appeared to be fresh blood, which had trickled from the corners of the mouth. Even the deep, burning eyes seemed set among swollen flesh, for the lids and pouches underneath were bloated. But there was no sign of movement, no reaction to the rude uncovering.

Breathing quickly now, in little moaning gasps of fear and loathing, Harker bent closer, forcing himself to examine his find carefully. Indeed, it seemed to Harker that the whole awful creature was simply gorged with blood—like a filthy leech, exhausted with his repletion.

Making a great effort of will, Harker bent still further over the man—the thing in the shape of a man—lying in the box of earth, and tried, in vain, to discover any sign of life. His hand on Dracula's chest could find no pulse, no breath, no beating of the heart.

In a moment Harker had nerved himself to search the ornate robe for pockets, hoping to discover keys—but without success. Looking closely into the dead eyes, Harker saw in them, unfocused though they were and unconscious of the intruder's presence, such a look of hate that the young man recoiled instinctively.

Even as he stepped back fear began to transform into anger.

This, *this* was the being he, Harker, was helping to transfer to London, where, perhaps, for centuries to come he might, among the teeming millions, satiate his lust for blood and create a new and ever-widening circle of semidemons to batten on the helpless. . . .

To London, where innocent, trusting Mina lived . . .

Reeling back from the open coffin, sobbing and moaning in his suddenly energized rage and fear, Harker grabbed up one of the shovels that stood handy, and was about to swing the metal edge with all his power against that pale, unliving face.

But at that moment the eyes abruptly altered in the undead face; the gaze of the count fell upon the one who threatened him, and seemed to rob the young man of his full strength.

The shovel dropped from Harker's hands to clatter on the broken pavement. Staggering back, he came up against the half-ruined mausoleum wall of individual burial vaults. Immediately he was caught at, pinched, by something—no, by several things—pale rootlike things that were attached to this wall, growing from it. . . . They grew out from the wall, and they caught at Harker's clothing; first one snag and then another.

Without comprehension he stared down at the fingers of a small, white hand that clutched his trouser leg.

In a shock of horror the young man realized that he had once more fallen into the seductive grasp of the three vampire women.

Now he could hear and recognize their sleepy, murmuring voices. Their six pale, bare arms were reaching out through the broken ends of their respective sepulchers to hold him. Their small fingers and their sharp nails were grasping drowsily, weakly, at his clothing, at his body.

Quite clearly he could hear and know the sweet tones of the youngest bride, murmuring seductively from within the vault.

"Don't leave usss—you want usss tonight—"

The laughter of the three brides tinkled.

He knew that he need only waver in his hard purpose for a

moment, and all the wicked delight he had experienced upon that soft moonlit bed would once again be his. . . .

Groaning incoherently, making a tremendous effort, Harker tore himself free. Now running for freedom almost blindly, avoiding the main entrance of the chapel where the Gypsies toiled, he sought the dim fading daylight visible from another direction, low down on a broken wall.

Squeezing his body through the narrow aperture, Harker ran, and fell, and crawled, and ran again.

And now, at last, he reached a place where there were no more stone walls, and he could feel clean rain upon his face. And where the only laughter to be heard was human. Crazy laughter, but quite human.

The laughter kept on and on. It stopped at last only because he needed all his breath to run.

8

Some weeks later, on a sultry day in early August, Renfield, the former lawyer in the firm of Hawkins and Thompkins, was growing increasingly uneasy in his cell in the asylum at Purfleet. Today even the cultivation of his many lives, his pets, the insects and arachnids and birds that he usually found completely fascinating, had ceased to hold the patient's interest.

All during the early hours of the warm afternoon Renfield had been riveted to the barred window of his cell, watching the sky, making no response to doctors or attendants who looked in on him, or to the occasional calls and outcries of his fellow inmates.

Just now the summer air in the vicinity of Purfleet was heavy and quiet, but the former solicitor could sense—just *how* Renfield was able to sense such things he could not have explained—that a mighty storm was approaching from the Channel. In his mind's eye he could perceive the gray clouds, their masses tinged with sunburst at the far edge, hanging over the gray sea. The fringe of the ocean came tumbling in over the shallows and the sandy flats with a roar, muffled in the sea mists drifting inland. The horizon out there was lost in a gray mist, all was vastness, the clouds were piled like giant rocks, and over the sea hung a murmuring like some presage of doom. Dark indistinguishable figures, sometimes half-shrouded in the mist, moved on the beaches.

What was stranger, much stranger, than the fact of the onrushing tempest, was that the tremendous storm was *controlled*. In Renfield's perception, it was as if Nature herself were being manipulated by a single, powerful hand. It was a hand whose identity the madman was sure he could recognize, that of the very Master whose coming Renfield had so long and eagerly awaited.

Naturally enough the oncoming tempest was driving ships racing before its winds. That in itself was only to be expected. But—

One ship in particular, a foreign sailing vessel, loomed up clearly in Renfield's perception. There was something very special about this craft; something in its cargo, yes, that was it—a kind of miracle all crated in the hold. . . .

But he dared not even think much about that now. Today the heavy air held glorious secrets, secrets that for the time being must be kept. . . .

Even after the passage of weeks, Renfield's bones still ached from the beating he had received at the hands of the attendants who had been trying to protect Dr. Seward from him. Poor Dr. Seward; he wasn't really Renfield's enemy.

No . . . there was really no benefit to be derived from strangling Dr. Seward.

The storm was coming. Closer now.

Renfield's arms and legs moved stiffly as at last he retreated from the window. It was high time, he thought, that he reviewed his cultivation of small lives in all the corners of his cell. Small indeed, but when properly accumulated, they could still be important.

Crouching on the floor, he murmured to his flies and spiders: "Gather 'round, my pets; the Master of all life will soon be at hand."

Thomas Bilder, senior keeper at the London Zoological Gardens adjoining Regent's Park, and a resident, with his wife, of one of the small cottages behind the elephant house, was proud to have in his charge the whole collection of wolves and jackals and hyenas.

Mr. Bilder's undoubted favorite among the animals was a huge gray wolf, called Berserker, more for its formidable size and appearance than for any actually demonstrated ferocity. On calm days, right after the wolf had finished feeding, the keeper would sometimes dare to scratch Berserker's ears. The beast had been captured four years ago in Norway, then had come to Jamrach's, a well-known London dealer in animals, and thence to the zoo.

Today Bilder, looking from a window of his cottage, took note of the oppressive atmosphere and the impending storm. He also heard several distant but penetrating howls and yelps suggesting that his animals were alarmed. Sometimes visitors did things to torment them. Grumbling to his wife, the keeper conscientiously decided to make an extra trip to the cages some four hundred yards away to examine the condition of his charges.

On arriving at the exhibit, Mr. Bilder observed that several wolves, in particular Berserker, were becoming increasingly excited by—as the keeper thought—the change of atmosphere. Given the ominous state of the weather, few visitors of any kind were present today, and none seemed to be bothering the animals.

Berserker on this particular afternoon happened to be alone in a cage, where he was restlessly trotting back and forth, howling and yelping almost continuously. Bilder spoke soothingly to the beast and tried to calm him—on this occasion, as the keeper later testified, he would not have thought of putting hand or arm inside the cage. But Berserker was not to be pacified, and Bilder, with other tasks demanding his attention, soon abandoned the effort.

Only moments after the keeper had turned away, the rain poured down, causing him to hasten his retreat in the direction of his cottage.

And only seconds after the onset of the rain, the storm's first bolt of lightning to strike in the vicinity of the zoo came ripping and rending its way down through the cage's iron bars and gate.

By great good fortune neither people nor animals were injured, but all restraints upon Berserker's freedom had been instantly and violently removed, the bars of the cage left twisted and melted open. Seconds later the gray shape of the wolf was seen bounding out and disappearing into the rainy park.

Despite the downpour, Bilder turned back when the lightning struck and was among the first to see the blasted cage. He attempted for several minutes to pursue the escaped animal, but again his efforts proved completely futile.

At the time of the wolf's escape in central London, the storm was still some minutes away from reaching Hillingham. This afternoon, Mina Murray and Lucy Westenra were seated together on a stone bench just below the formal garden, right along the border of the family cemetery, which formed a peaceful and familiar part of the estate's enormous parklike grounds.

The day had been sleepy and quiet, except for the occasional peacock's cry. Early morning had been bright with sunshine, but since midday the sky had grown increasingly cloudy, until now the weather in the east seemed downright ominous. But at the moment neither young woman was paying much attention to the sky.

Lucy, drawing a deep breath, taking in the familiar scene, announced to her companion: "Oh, this is my favorite spot in all the world—"

Mina thought that she could detect a false note in this cheerful assessment. "But something is bothering you?"

"Not really. No." Lucy's gaze became remote. "It's just that I've lately begun sleepwalking again—you know, as I did when we were girls. And, Mina, I have the strangest dreams!"

"You're not having a sordid affair with a tall, dark stranger?"

Lucy smiled. "What a delicious suggestion—but no. The truth is that I love him! I love him! There, it does me good to say it. I love him and I've said yes!"

"Oh, Lucy, finally!" Mina's happiness for her friend was tinged with jealousy. "You've made your choice, then. Is it to be the Texan with the big knife?"

Even as Mina asked her question thunder began a distant rumbling in the east.

Lucy shook her red curls. "No. I'm afraid Quincey's now disappointed, just as Jack was. Arthur's the one I've chosen. Oh, Mina, eventually Arthur and I'll be Lord and Lady Godalming, and next summer you'll visit us at our villa in France. You and Jonathan, I mean. And of course you are to be my maid of honor—oh, say yes!"

"Of course I will, Luce . . . but I really thought you loved that Texas creature."

Lucy looked around, surprised, as at a misunderstanding. "But I do—and I shall continue to love him."

"And Dr. Seward also, I suppose."

"Yes, brilliant Doctor Jack, who so nicely asked for my hand—why not? Don't look at me that way, Mina. If, after I am married, the chance should arise for me to be with one of them . . . honestly you can be so naive about these things! So uncivilized. You've been an absolute bore ever since Jonathan went abroad—oh, I'm sorry, dear! Forgive me?"

Mina was suddenly weeping.

Lucy, her own affairs momentarily forgotten, was all sympathy and concern. "But you're worried about Jonathan. Of course you are!"

"It's just . . . just that I've had only two letters in all this time. One from Paris, and one from—where he's staying. And his last letter was so unnatural, so cold. Not like Jonathan at all."

There came a vivid split of lightning in the east, and thunder crashed again, louder this time. During the last few minutes the sky over the river had become quite threatening, and now a chill wind began to stir from that direction.

"Mina—are you sure you really know him?" Flash and crash in the sky again. "All men can be like that, you know, untrustworthy—"

Lucy's last words were lost in thunder. By mutual consent the girls arose from the bench and began to move toward the house.

"Not Jonathan—" Mina was shaking her dark curls.

"Jonathan, too, believe me, dear." Lucy nodded wisely. "But if he's turning cold, it could be that you're in love with the wrong man—"

The rain came drenching down, soaking the young women's dresses as they ran. The storm with its unnatural power drove them helplessly before it.

Out in the Channel, the schooner *Demeter,* of Russian registration, had been for many hours running before the high wind under full sail. This apparent recklessness on the part of captain and crew, marveled at by some observers on shore who saw the vessel's approach, was later partially explained in a most gruesome way.

The ship, after being driven violently into the mouth of the Thames, finally ran aground near Greenwich, and investigators on going aboard found all hands but the steersman missing. And that individual, later ascertained to be also the captain, was mysteriously dead, his hands lashed to the wheel.

In the corpse's pocket was a bottle, carefully corked, empty save for a little roll of paper, which, when later translated—rather clumsily—by a clerk at the Russian embassy, proved to be an addendum to the ship's log, the remainder of which the clerk also rendered into English. The translation created a stir when it was printed in several of the more sensation-oriented London newspapers.

Another twist to the *Demeter*'s most peculiar story, soon picked up by the newspapers, was provided by several witnesses of the grounding. These all agreed that a giant dog, springing up from somewhere belowdecks, had been seen to leap ashore from the prow of the vessel the instant after she had struck the dock. A search was soon instituted for this animal, but it could not be found.

As for the dead man at the wheel, he was simply fastened by his hands, tied one over the other, to one of the spokes. Between the inner hand and the wood was a crucifix, the set of beads on which it was fastened being looped around both wrists and wheel, and kept fast there by the binding cords.

A surgeon, J. M. Caffyn, upon making an examination, declared that the man must have been dead for quite two days; and a coast guard declared it possible that the victim might have tied up his own hands, drawing the knots tight with his teeth. Needless to say, the dead steersman was soon removed from the place where, as the newspaper accounts described it, "he had held his honorable watch and ward till death," and was placed in a mortuary to await inquest.

Of course the verdict at the captain's inquest was an open one. Whether or not he himself, in a state of madness, might have murdered his entire crew, there was no one to say. Popular opinion held almost universally that the captain of the *Demeter* was simply a hero, and he was given a public funeral.

The cargo of the *Demeter* was found to consist almost entirely of fifty large wooden boxes containing earth, or mold. These had been consigned to a London solicitor, Mr. S. F. Billington, who on the morning after the ship's grounding went aboard and formally took possession of the goods. Billington's client, doing business by mail, had already paid him well, for privacy and efficiency, and instructed him as to where the boxes were to be shipped next. Most, though the newspapers never discovered this, were bound for an apparently abandoned estate called Carfax.

A good deal of interest was abroad concerning the dog that bounded ashore when the ship struck, and more than a few members of the SPCA, the Society for the Prevention of Cruelty to Animals, wanted to befriend the animal. To the general disappointment, however, it was not to be found.

At the height of the storm, near the hour when the *Demeter* had run aground, many of the inmates at Seward's asylum grew violently restless, and their keepers employed a high-pressure water hose to subdue the most rebellious. For once Renfield was not among the malcontents—ignoring the outcries of his fellow patients in their cells, he remained, for the time being, seemingly content to cultivate in peace his multitude of small subhuman lives.

By midnight, the rain at Hillingham had almost entirely ceased, but great gusts of moaning wind still hurled clusters of ragged clouds across the sky, set trees dancing all across the parklike grounds, and rattled windows.

At that hour Mina, roused by some gust or crash of weather louder than the rest—or perhaps by some more subtle cause—got out of her bed and, feeling instinctively uneasy, went into Lucy's bedroom, which adjoined her own.

Nervously she whispered: "Lucy—are you all right?"

In the heavy darkness, the bed just in front of Mina was almost invisible.

She tried again, a little louder. "Lucy . . . ?"

Still no answer.

Moving forward, the young woman groped over and among the disarranged sheets and coverlet and pillows. The bed was certainly unoccupied, and the bedclothes felt cool; Lucy had evidently been out of them for some time.

Suddenly the octagonal window that gave on the terrace blew open, and the curtains were dancing. In the act of closing the window and fastening it again, Mina to her astonishment caught a glimpse, in one of the faint flashes of the now-receding storm, of Lucy's small figure, unmistakable in her red nightgown, moving away from the house and already at a considerable distance, descending the broad low flight of steps that led to the family cemetery.

Sleepwalking again!

Darting quickly back to her own room, Mina hastily threw on some clothes over her own nightgown—then picked up a big, heavy shawl, for Lucy, and ran out to the rescue.

The wind continued wet and chill, still scouring patches of fog up from the river. Swift-flying clouds alternately hid and revealed the moon. The worried young woman had not very far to go in her search. There, unmistakable in a moment of bright moonlight, was Lucy again. She was seated on the familiar stone bench, but this time sprawled wantonly back upon it.

But it was a sight far more shocking that froze Mina in her tracks.

Writhing right over Lucy's supine body, actually between her spread thighs, there crouched a black shape the size of a large man—though Mina in her shock and dread could not be certain whether the form she saw was that of man or beast. Above the intermittent wind a kind of howling, sighing outcry came from one of the figures on the bench. A sound as of a woman moaning in soft hopeless pain; either in pain, as Mina thought to herself in horror, or else—

Breaking whatever spell had for an instant held her back, Mina strode bravely forward. "Lucy! Luucyyy . . ."

At the sound of her voice the dark form reared up frighteningly, turned, and looked at Mina. Or at least it seemed to her that its red eyes were looking directly at her, eyes so red and fiercely glowing that she wondered for an instant how she could have imagined that it was indeed a man.

And then a cloud covered the moon again, and in the darkness a man's voice spoke directly to Mina, a voice so low as to be almost inaudible. The voice was saying something to her—no, it was entreating, no, commanding something of her—in a foreign tongue, using words Mina had never heard before, but yet could understand.

And the man's voice spoke a name—*Elisabeth.*

Elisabeth, do not see me. A command, and it was obeyed—because Mina had just seen that which she did not wish to see . . .

. . . Only a moment later the moonlight, coming back, showed Lucy still sprawled on the bench, but quite alone. (And Mina thought to herself: Am I mad? Why do I have the feeling that a moment ago she was *not* alone? Yet there is no one with her!)

And a good thing, too, for Lucy's nightdress, her only garment, was shamefully, obscenely disarranged. She was breathing in long, heavy gasps.

Mina, murmuring and crying in sympathy, hastened to her friend, first rearranging Lucy's nightgown decently, then adding, for both warmth and propriety, the heavy shawl, which she fastened with a safety pin at her friend's throat.

Removing her own shoes, she slipped them on the girl's bare feet. Then she lifted Lucy, who was still moaning, only semiconscious, from the bench, got her on her feet, and began leading her back toward the house.

Halfway there, the girl in Mina's arms stumbled and partially awakened.

As if in muffled terror, Lucy murmured: "His eyes . . . his eyes . . ."

"It's all right." Mina was trying to soothe her friend, and to keep her moving at the same time. "You were dreaming, dear. Walking in your sleep again. That's all."

Lucy moaned weakly. "Please don't tell anyone—please. It would kill Mother."

"I shan't tell anyone."

They were crossing the terrace now, treading the wet pavement among leaves and twigs ripped down by the storm. Ahead of them the familiar house loomed strangely in the foggy night.

"Lucy—who is Elisabeth? I have the feeling . . ." And an indescribably strange feeling it was, as if she, Mina, had very recently heard someone—someone she seemed to know very well— call her by that name.

"Mina?" Lucy was lost in confusion, obviously with no idea even of what the question was about.

"Never mind." Mina led her briskly on. "Never mind. We must get you back to bed."

Elisabeth . . .

It was no command this time, and therefore it went unheard. It was only a marveling sigh, uttered by the far traveler who watched from the cemetery, himself invisible in darkness and in rain.

EXCERPTS FROM LOG OF THE *DEMETER*
Varna to London

13 July. Passed Cape Matapan. Crew (five hands, two mates, cook) seemed dissatisfied about something. Seemed scared, but would not speak out.

14 July. Somewhat anxious about crew. Men all steady fellows who have sailed with me before. Mate could not make out what was wrong; they only told him there was *something*, and crossed themselves. Mate lost temper with one of them and struck him. Expected fierce quarrel, but all was quiet.

16 July. Mate reported in the morning that one of crew, Petrofsky, was missing. Could not account for it. Took larboard watch eight bells last night; was relieved by Abramoff, but did not go to bunk. Men more downcast than ever. All said they expected something of the kind, but would not say any more than that there was

something aboard. Mate getting very impatient with them. Fear some trouble ahead.

17 July. One of the men, Olgaren, came to my cabin and in an awestruck way confided to me he thought there was a strange man aboard the ship. He said that in his watch he saw a tall, thin man, who was not like any of the crew, come up the companionway and go along the deck forward and disappear.

Later in the day I got together the whole crew and told them, as they evidently thought there was someone in the ship, we would search from stem to stern. I let mate take helm while the rest began thorough search, all keeping abreast, with lanterns. As there were only the big wooden boxes, there were no odd corners where a man could hide. Men much relieved when search over, and went back to work cheerfully.

22 July. Rough weather last three days, and all hands busy with sails. No time to be frightened. Men seem to have forgotten their dread. Mate cheerful again, and all on good terms. Passed Gibraltar and out through straits. All well.

24 July. There seems some doom over this ship. Already a hand short, and entering Bay of Biscay with wild weather ahead, and yet another man lost—disappeared. Like the first, he came off his watch and was not seen again. Men all in a panic, asking to have double watch, as they fear to be alone. Mate violent. Fear there will be some trouble, as either he or the men will do some violence.

28 July. Four days in hell, the wind a tempest. No sleep for anyone. Men all worn-out. Hardly know how to set a watch, since no one fit to go on. Second mate volunteered to steer and watch, and let men snatch a few hours' sleep. Wind abating, seas still terrific.

29 July. Another tragedy. Had single watch tonight, as crew too tired to double. When morning watch came on deck could find no one except steersman. Raised outcry, and all came on deck. Thorough search, but no one found. Are now without second mate, and crew in a panic. Mate and I agreed to go armed henceforth and wait for any sign of cause.

30 July. Rejoice we are nearing England. Weather fine, all sails set. Retired worn-out, slept soundly, awakened by mate telling me both man of watch and steersman missing. Only self and mate and two hands left to work ship.

1 August. Two days of fog, and not a sail sighted. Had hoped when in the English Channel to be able to signal for help or get in somewhere. Not having power to work sails, have to run before wind. Dare not lower, as could not raise them again.

Mate now more demoralized than either of men. Men are beyond fear, working stolidly and patiently, with minds made up to worst.

2 August, midnight. Woke up from few minutes' sleep by cry, seemingly outside my port. Rushed on deck, could see nothing in fog, ran against mate. Tells me heard cry and ran, but no sign of man on watch. One more gone. We may be in Straits of Dover or even in North Sea. Only God can guide us in this fog, which seems to move with us; and God seems to have deserted us.

3 August. At midnight went to relieve man at wheel, but when I got to it found no one there. I dared not leave it, so shouted for the mate.
     After a few seconds he rushed up on deck. I greatly fear his reason has given way. He came close to me and whispered hoarsely: "*It* is here! On watch last night I saw it, like a man, tall, thin, ghastly pale, I crept behind it, and gave it my knife; but the knife went through it, empty as the air.
     "But it is here, and I'll find it. In the hold perhaps, in one of those boxes. I'll unscrew them one by one. You work the helm." And with a warning look, and his finger on his lip, he went below.
     There was springing up a choppy wind, and I could not leave the helm. I saw the mate come out on deck again with a tool chest and a lantern, and go down the forward hatchway. He is stark raving mad, and no use my trying to stop him. He can't hurt those big boxes, they are invoiced as clay, and to pull them about is as harmless a thing as he can do. So here I stay, and mind the helm, and write these notes. I can only trust in God, and wait till the fog clears. . . .
     It is nearly all over now. Just as I was beginning to hope the mate would come out calmer, there came up the hatchway a scream, and up on the deck he came as if shot from a gun.
     "Save me! Save me!" he cried, and looked around on the blanket of fog. His horror turned to despair, and in a steady voice he said: "You better come, too, Captain, before it is too late. *He* is there, but the sea will save me from him!" Before I could say a word, he sprang on the bulwark and threw himself into the sea.
     I suppose I know the secret now. It was this madman who got rid of the men one by one, and now he has followed them himself. God help me!

4 August. Still fog, which sunrise cannot pierce. I dared not go below, I dared not leave the helm. So here all night I stayed, and in the dimness of the night I saw it—him! God forgive me, but the mate was right to jump overboard. Better to die like a man, to die

like a sailor in blue water, no one can object. But I am captain, and must not leave my ship. I shall tie my hands to the wheel when my strength begins to fail, and with them tie that which he—it!—dares not touch. If we are wrecked, mayhap this bottle may be found, and those who find it may understand. . . .

9

On the day after Lucy's latest sleepwalking escapade, Mina ordered a carriage—trains were readily available, but her wealthy friends insisted on being generous in such matters—and went into town. In the smoke and clamor and excitement of the city Mina endeavored to distract herself from her continued worry about Jonathan as well as her new concern for Lucy. She also took the opportunity to make a few essential purchases.

On Piccadilly and the Strand newsboys were loudly hawking papers: SUDDENEST AND GREATEST STORM ON RECORD STRIKES ENGLAND—ESCAPED WOLF FROM ZOO STILL AT LARGE— But their shouts scarcely distracted the young woman at all.

The day was only moderately foggy, for London; but even had the weather been perfectly clear, Mina would have given little thought to her immediate surroundings.

Thus it was that for several hours she had no idea that she was being followed.

Heavy feeding, during the voyage and afterward, had restored to him the outward appearance of youth, as he had known it would. And today he had a strong wish to appear young; for today, after more than four hundred years of separation, he would at last, if the fates were kind, once more stand face-to-face with Elisabeth. . . .

The visitor to London who followed Mina without her knowledge was dressed in the height of fashion, including an elegant top hat, but before the day was far advanced he wished he had chosen headwear with a broader brim to go with his fashionable dark glasses. The fact was that he required a certain amount of protection against even this foggy northern variety of daylight.

To move thus, wincing at occasional direct sunbeams, through the unfamiliar streets of a large, modern city, was a new experience for him, but today he gave the adventure only incidental attention. His urgent desire was to approach this particular young woman openly by day, and in a manner impeccably civilized, if not strictly correct according to the local social codes.

A thousand wild hopes, incoherent and fantastic, churned in the visitor's heart. Hopes that were based on a woman's face glimpsed only in a photograph, and then once more, directly, in recent time—seen only very briefly, and at night, and by sheer miraculous chance—but then, could there be, really, truly, any such thing as sheer chance in the affairs of star-crossed men and women?

There she went, crossing the Strand. . . . With an effortlessness born of centuries of experience the hunter stalked his quarry among the crowds.

At last, having deftly maneuvered himself into a position in the moving throng where she would be able to see him clearly, he murmured, almost inaudibly: "My love . . . see me now."

And somehow, as tense and preoccupied as Mina Murray was, in the midst of her concentration upon her worries and her errands, the message was silently conveyed.

Her eyes met the unfamiliar gaze of her pursuer—he was just, at that moment, removing his dark glasses—and like any well-bred young woman of her time and place she immediately looked away.

But then something compelled Mina to glance again at the well-dressed, youthful-looking man, his glossy brown hair hanging to his shoulders.

Disturbed more deeply than the incident seemed to warrant, she broke off eye contact—this time, as she thought, for good—and entered an apothecary shop.

Impatiently Dracula crossed the street to look in through the shop window, avoiding the common obstacles of pedestrian traffic by movement at speeds and in ways available to no ordinary human.

None of the many people who hurried past along the pavement, intent upon their own affairs, took notice of these movements, nor did they observe that the window did not reflect the young man's image; it only mirrored, rather faintly, the newspaper he was holding, with its front-page stories about the storm and the escaped wolf.

Inside the shop, Mina was concentrating for the moment upon her purchase of a bottle of laudanum—the tincture of opium and alcohol, commonly available, might be just what Lucy needed to fight the tendency toward sleepwalking; and Mina's own worries about Jonathan were keeping her awake nights, too.

As Mina emerged from the shop the one who had been following, staring at her hungrily, able to hear her soft voice even through the thick glass window—that one intercepted her, his sudden immediate presence startling her so much that she dropped the bottle.

Swiftly and gracefully he caught the fragile glass out of the air. Politely he held it out.

"My humblest apologies," he murmured, in his lightly accented English—not nearly so accented as it had been a few months past. "I am recently arrived from abroad and do not know your city. Is a beautiful lady permitted to give a lost soul directions?"

Mina put out her hand, on the verge of accepting the bottle, then hesitated absently; her eyes were probing at the figure before her, puzzled by some hint of familiarity . . . but the first command he had given her—*Do not see me!*—had been strong enough to make it—almost—impossible to overcome.

Her first conscious response to this bold stranger was quite cool. "For lost souls I would suggest any of our many churches. And I believe that sixpence will purchase a street guide—good day."

With that Mina began to turn away—only to realize that the stranger's white-gloved hand was still in possession of her medicine. She turned back.

Once more he offered the dark liquid. "Laudanum, I see." Though he had not really looked at the package. "Forgetfulness in a bottle. For a sick friend, no doubt?"

"That is hardly your business."

The stranger managed to seem confident and contrite at the same time. "Now I have offended you. But I am only looking for the cinematograph; I understand it is the wonder of the civilized world."

"If you seek culture, visit a museum. London is filled with them. If you will excuse me?"

He bowed politely, touching his hat's brim, and courteously allowed her to pass.

But before Mina had walked many yards, she entered a patch

of denser fog and encountered him again. How could he *possibly* have gotten ahead of her so fast on the crowded pavement?

Again he touched his hat. "A woman so lovely should not be walking the streets of London alone. I even fear it may not be safe."

Mina walked on, ignoring him. She was astounded at the degree of effort that was required to do so.

He offered his arm, but the offer was ostentatiously declined. Undeterred, he fell smoothly into step beside her.

Mina, angry, stopped.

"I most certainly will not allow myself to be . . ." Inexplicably, as she met this stranger's eyes, her anger weakened; lamely she concluded: ". . . to be escorted by any gentleman who has not been properly introduced."

Or was he a stranger, truly? Certainly something about this man was exerting a tremendous attraction.

He smiled at her. "Such impertinence. I am really not accustomed to it. How refreshing! A quality that could cost you your life in my homeland."

"Then I should hope never to visit."

Dracula laughed appreciatively, delighted with her spirit.

"Do I know you, sir?" There was now a growing desperation in Mina's attitude. "Are you acquainted with my husband? Shall I call the police?"

The stranger's smile broadened at the sequence of questions; then it went away, leaving him quietly serious, perhaps even chastened.

He said: "Forgive my manner of rudeness. I am but a stranger in a strange land—*you must not fear me.*" The last five words were delivered softly but with great emphasis.

"Sir . . . I . . . perhaps I am the one who has been rude."

"Please, permit me to introduce myself. I believe I can perform the ritual properly to your satisfaction. I am Prince Vladislaus of Szeklys."

"What an . . . unusual name."

"And what a meaningless title. I am sure your London is filled with princes, dukes, sheikhs, and counts. In fact I am your humble servant." Taking off his hat momentarily, Dracula used it in a sweeping bow.

"Wilhelmina Murray . . ." Almost dazedly, Mina began a curtsy. A grip on her elbow, gentle but rock solid, kept her from completing the movement.

He was shaking his head. "It is I who am honored, Madam Mina."

"Madam . . . ?"

"You mentioned a husband."

"Did I . . . ?"

Her hand—*Elisabeth's hand!*—was on his arm as the two of them strolled away into the London fog.

Great bells—there, booming below the others, was the one they called Big Ben—beat in his ears. The exuberant life of the great city, the great world, surrounded him. On this day of joy all things seemed possible, even, perhaps, an ultimate reconciliation with life itself. . . .

Lucy was ill; and whatever the thing was that had infected her, it was beyond Jack Seward's power to diagnose. But it looked serious, damned serious in fact, all the more so because it had come upon the young woman so very suddenly.

Seward, summoned away from his interesting lunatics by a hastily written note from the worried Arthur Holmwood, could be sure of little more than that as he watched the woman to whom he had so recently proposed undergo a fitting of the dress in which she was soon to marry another man.

Though undeniably not well, Lucy seemed at the moment happy—with a kind of brittle excitement—and even energetic. Showing off the dress, she turned before a large mirror.

"Jack—brilliant Doctor Jack—do you like it?"

"Most elegant."

In fact, Lucy's visitor had hardly glanced at the dress, except to note that a worried-looking seamstress was having to take it in. Lucy's weight loss, just in the past few days, had been considerable. Her skin was now a chalky white, blotched with red at her lips and on her sunken cheeks. When she smiled, Seward could see how her gums had receded from the white teeth.

She swirled again. "So tell me, Doctor Jack—did Arthur put you up to this visit? Or did you just want me alone in my bed once before I'm married?"

He cleared his throat. "Lucy, Arthur is very worried about you. He has asked that I see you, as a physician. I realize this may be awkward for both of us, because there have been personal matters between us in the past. But that must not be allowed to . . . if I am to be your physician, I must have your complete trust."

Lucy was shaking her head, refusing, denying something—not necessarily what the doctor had just been saying. Suddenly weak and giddy, she dismissed the seamstress with a wave of her hand and sank down on a couch nearby, fingering the black velvet choker she was wearing around her neck.

"What is it, Lucy?"

"Help me, Jack—please, I don't know what's happening to me. I can't sleep at night. I have nightmares . . . I hear things I shouldn't be able to hear—"

That caught at Seward's professional curiosity. "What things?"

"It's idiotic." The patient tried to smile.

"Tell me anyway."

"I can hear servants whispering, clear away at the other end of the house. I hear mice way up in the attic—my mother's poor sick heart beating, in another room. And I can *see* things in the dark, Jack, as plain as day."

"Lucy . . ."

"And I'm—starving—but I cannot bear the sight of food— please, help me—"

Lucy gasped, bending forward, clutching at Seward, who in alarm had hastened to her side.

An hour later Seward's latest patient had been put to bed in her room, her ailing, worried mother comforted and deceived with some story about a slight indisposition. And now Seward, having concluded his preliminary examination, was walking in the great hall, conferring with Arthur Holmwood.

The prospective bridegroom, accompanied by Quincey Morris, had arrived at Hillingham a few minutes ago, both men in excellent spirits, wearing their hunting clothes. The good spirits did not last long. Holmwood in particular was naturally upset at the latest developments.

When he came out of Lucy's room after a quick visit, he was even more upset. "Jack, what do you make of it? To me it's frightening."

The physician sighed. "There seems no functional disturbance, or any malady that I can recognize. At the same time I am not satisfied with her appearance."

"I should think not!"

"So I have taken the liberty of cabling Abraham Van Helsing."

Holmwood was vaguely impressed by this announcement, but uncertain. "You mean your old teacher, Jack, of whom you speak so often? The Dutch metaphysician-philosopher?"

"Yes. The point is that he is also a physician, and that he knows more about obscure diseases than any other man in the world."

"Then do it, man, bring him here. Spare no expense."

Mina's planned return from town to Hillingham had been considerably delayed. Much against what would have been her better judgment—somehow the operation of that faculty seemed to have been suspended—she was on her way to attend the cinematograph with a man who had simply accosted her on the street. There was really no other word to describe the nature of their meeting.

Sunset over London was, as so often, filled with a wonderful smoky beauty, with its lurid lights and inky shadows and all the marvelous tints that come on foul clouds even as on foul water. As the red disk sank, the beauty it had produced faded into the late-coming darkness of spring. And Mina, clinging to the arm of her new escort, almost blindly, almost helplessly, had allowed him to bring her to an early, primitive motion-picture theater, the cinematograph.

The silent, black-and-white images currently on the screen, scratchy and jumpy, depicted a great gray wolf, which leaped repeatedly at the bars of its cage. Evidently the animal was being encouraged or tormented by some man who stood just out of the camera's range; at intervals his arm and hand appeared on screen, caught at the termination of some violent gesture. The small audience included well-to-do folk, mingling with the lower classes, even as they might on the street. The theater's customers stood or sat in a few rows of chairs, watching spellbound.

Dracula stood for some time with Mina at one side of the room, observing the images intently, as in the flick of an eyelash the gray wavering image of the wolf was succeeded by the silent onrush of a locomotive.

Impressed, Mina's companion commented: "Astounding. There are no limits to science."

"Is this science? I think it can hardly be compared with the work of Madame Curie." The screen had been unable to hold

Mina's attention for more than a few seconds. She was becoming increasingly nervous. "I shouldn't have come here. I must go. . . ."

"Not yet."

"But—"

His finger on her lips commanded her to silence. Then, with a firm hand on her arm, he guided her toward the rear of the little theater, through a set of heavy curtains, across a shabby little hallway, into a dark area almost immediately behind the large suspended screen. All during their progress to this isolated place Mina attempted to pull back, to protest.

"No, I can't—" To her own astonishment, she seemed unable to raise her voice above a whisper. "Please, stop this—who are you?"

When it seemed that Mina, throwing reserve and caution to the winds, might have cried out, Dracula's gloved hand came up to gently cover her mouth.

His voice compelled. It almost hypnotized. "You are as safe with me as you will ever be."

The gigantic black-and-white shadows of the images projected on the other side loomed over them. Here came Queen Victoria, first small and then enormous in a royal carriage, part of a silent procession celebrating Her Majesty's diamond jubilee.

The audience, invisible on the front side of the screen, offered Her Majesty respectful applause.

Carefully Dracula let his companion go. Her eyes were closed, her lips moved, but almost silently. He realized that she was praying.

He whispered softly: "You are she, the love of my life. The one I have lost and found again."

And even as he spoke the words, he felt the blood-lust, the raw hunger, rising, the fangs in his own jaw extending like erectile tissue—but not with Elisabeth! NO!

In dismay, astonishment at this spontaneous rebellion of his own nature, he turned his countenance away. Fiercely he exerted his will for a long moment. Before he turned back to his beloved, his face, his mouth were human once again.

Mina, though he felt sure she could not have seen the brief transformation, was trembling in fear. "My God—*who are you?*"

He, too, was quivering with emotion. "For you, I am only good."

Frightened, bewitched, confused, she could only stare at him, not understanding. Not even beginning to understand.

And at that moment, fearful of discovery, afraid of her own

nature, looking over the shoulder of the incredible, inexplicable man who held her, Mina Murray found herself gazing into the bright blue eyes of a real wolf.

There was a half-open door, a real and shabby wooden door, just behind the wolf, and with part of her mind Mina realized that this must be the escaped animal from the zoo, and that it must have made its way through the city by mews and alleys and byways, and come stalking into the rear of the theater through some door or window that had accidentally been left open.

Her escort had now become aware of what stood behind him. He let go of Mina and turned to look at the beast.

At that moment Mina, stricken by sudden panic, deprived of the support his hands and his gaze had given her, turned to run.

The wolf, more in fright than in ferocity, sprang after her.

Dracula's voice, a whipcrack syllable or two in some tongue that Mina had never heard before, stopped the animal almost in mid-leap.

It cowered, almost whimpering, as if it not only understood but was somehow compelled to obey.

Meanwhile in the background the gigantic images continued their silent dance on the reversed screen, their lights and shadows flickering over the beast and the two people.

Dracula, calm and matter-of-fact, crouched and beckoned gently to the wolf. Head down, obedient, the animal came to him.

He cradled Berserker's head in his white gloves, rubbing the beast's ears, stroking its great back.

Then the man raised his eyes to those of his human companion. "Come here, Mina. I tell you to have no fear."

Mina resisted at first, shaking her head wildly.

Dracula arose. Quietly he took her by the hand, pulling her easily and steadily to the wolf, which at her first approach put back its ears like a great cat. But then the animal relaxed.

Petting the wolf, safely, her fingers meeting those of her companion in the animal's thick fur, she found herself intoxicated, enchanted, full of trust.

Two hours later, a hired coach deposited a shaken and transformed Mina at the front portico of Hillingham.

No words had been exchanged during the last five minutes of ride. As soon as her companion—her new lover—had helped her to alight, Mina, without allowing time for any speech, turned her back on man and coach and literally ran toward the house.

When she had almost reached the door, an irresistible impulse stopped her, and she turned back for one more yearning, agonizing look. But the coach and the man who had ridden in it with her were already gone.

10

The lights at Hillingham were once more burning into the morning hours. In one of the upstairs rooms of the huge house Dr. Seward was still keeping watch at Lucy's bedside.

Seward took his patient's pulse yet again, shook his head unhappily, and quietly left the sickroom to stretch his legs a little in the hall; to try to keep awake, and try to think.

At that moment a hired cab pulled up at the main entrance of Hillingham. The man who alighted from the vehicle was well into middle age, and of good stature, a figure of solid dignity. He was carrying a good-sized medical bag—after a hurried journey from Amsterdam across the Channel, he had left most of his luggage at the Berkeley Hotel in central London.

Having paid and dismissed his transportation, Abraham Van Helsing stood for a moment blinking, considering the great house as if its few lighted windows, all on upper floors, might be able to tell him something meaningful about its occupants.

With the departure of Dr. Seward from her room, Lucy was for the moment left quite alone.

But only for a moment. Somehow becoming aware of a silent, shadowy, and ominous presence hovering on the terrace, just outside the French doors, the young woman suddenly awakened. Gone was the extreme debility and weariness that Seward had noted in her sleeping countenance only a few minutes ago; now Lucy looked energetic, even joyful.

Her eyes brightened. Smiling wantonly at the entity that was only vaguely visible beyond the glass, she provocatively drew back the bedclothes.

* * *

Seward, alerted by a sleepy servant to the fact of Van Helsing's arrival, came hurrying downstairs to find his old mentor just shedding his hat, gloves, and overcoat in the front hall.

The younger man, vastly relieved, almost ran forward, both hands extended in greeting. "Professor, how good of you to come!"

"I come to my friend in need when he calls!" And the visitor prolonged the handclasp, studying Seward carefully. In a moment Van Helsing's own expression had become grave; he could see easily enough that social niceties and reminiscences had better be postponed.

Without preliminary he demanded: "Jack, tell me everything about your case."

Running weary fingers through his hair, Seward tersely recited a preliminary list of Lucy's symptoms and the tests he had already performed.

He concluded: "She has all the usual physical anemic signs. Her blood analyzes normal—and yet it is not. She manifests continued blood loss—but I cannot trace the cause."

Van Helsing had barely started to frame his next question when a wild orgasmic wail sounded from upstairs.

The two men looked at each other in surprise, then wordlessly ran for the stairs. Seward was in the lead, with Van Helsing, still carrying his medical bag, puffing somewhat to keep up. Even as they went pounding up the stairs Lucy's loud wanton moans continued, then broke off abruptly in a kind of climax.

Moments later the pair of physicians, Seward still leading the way, burst into her room.

Van Helsing, on entering, stopped in his tracks. *"Gott in Himmel!"*

The French window now stood open, the curtains blowing in the chill draft. Lucy, almost completely naked, lay sprawled on her back across the bed. A small pool of blood was caking on her pillow, and her bosom heaved as she struggled to draw breath.

Van Helsing moved immediately to the bedside, where he examined the patient's body for a bleeding wound. He took note especially of the throat, from which the black choker she wore had now been removed. The professor drew up the bedclothes to cover the young woman decently and warmly.

Then he turned to confront Seward, even as the younger man

came back from closing the door to the terrace, making sure that it was latched securely and drawing the curtains back into place across it.

"There is no time to be lost," Van Helsing informed his colleague firmly. He looked as grimly determined as Seward had ever seen him. "There must be transfusion of blood at once."

Even as he spoke the professor was opening his medical bag, which he had already set down on the bed.

Seward, lighting one of several candles that were standing ready at the bedside, looked up, surprised at this proposal. "Transfusion? You've perfected the procedure?"

"Perfected?" Van Helsing shook his head. "No one has done that yet. I've only experimented, using Landsteiner's method. It is true that the risk is very great, but we have no choice. This woman will die tonight if we do nothing."

Belatedly commotion was building out in the hall. Alarm had spread among the servants, and a pair of maids carrying lamps now put their frightened faces into the bedroom.

Swiftly Seward issued orders to the servants and sent them away with the additional warning not to awaken Lucy's mother. Meanwhile Van Helsing was pulling from his bag the implements required to perform the contemplated operation—some lengths of rubber tubing, so thin-walled as to be practically transparent; two heavy needles, some auxiliary equipment, including a small hand-operated pump.

The younger doctor, busily arranging a chair, tables, and lamps about the bed, observed this activity with continued surprise.

"You came prepared to perform a transfusion, Professor?"

His mentor nodded grimly. "*Ja*. From what you told me in your cable, I suspected. Now the need is certain."

New footsteps, these heavier and almost running, sounded in the hall. In another moment Arthur Holmwood, in his hat and topcoat, had appeared at the door of Lucy's bedroom.

Arthur—who, as Seward realized, must have just come from the bedside of his dying father, Lord Godalming—took in the scene with shock and wonder. Lucy's betrothed stared without understanding at the two men in her room. He took in the pale, slight figure in the bed, the already bloodstained sheets and pillow. The multiple strains on Arthur's nerves threatened to overcome him.

"What the bloody hell?" Holmwood grated, pushing forward. "What are you doing to my Lucy?"

Seward hastily intervened. "Art, this is Van Helsing, the specialist. He's trying to save her, old chap." Quickly he performed a more formal introduction.

Van Helsing, fully occupied with the medical struggle he was about to undertake, only glanced up, nodding instead of offering to shake hands. His face looked grim and tough.

"Ah, the fiancé," he grunted. "You've come in good time. This young lady is very ill. She wants blood, and blood she must have. Take off your coat." Arthur barely hesitated, but even an instant's delay was too much for Van Helsing. He barked again: "Take off your coat!"

The overcoat and hat came off at once. Holmwood was shaken now, apologetic. "Forgive me, sir. My life is hers. I would give my last drop of blood to save her."

Van Helsing showed his teeth in a kind of smile. "I do not ask as much as that—yet. But come! You are a man, and it is a man we want." With a fierce gesture he pointed to the chair at the bedside.

"Jack was to give his blood"—this was news to Seward, who looked up sharply; the younger doctor had not yet begun to consider by what process a donor might be chosen—"as he is more young and strong than me. But now you are here, you are better than us, who toil in the world of thought. Our nerves are not so calm and our blood not so bright than yours!"

Obviously, Seward observed admiringly, the professor had been profoundly energized, elated by this postmidnight challenge, coming after what must have been a tiring trip across the Channel. He was proceeding with his preparations, now holding up the two large, sharp, hollow needles, one in each hand, connected by an apparatus of rubber tubing and the bulb pump.

His chuckle had something sadistic in it.

Seward, meanwhile, had stripped the bewildered Holmwood of his inner coat, ripped up his shirt sleeve, sat him down in the chair at bedside, tied off his arm, and thumped up a vein.

Now, swiftly but with absolute method, Van Helsing performed the operation.

As he inserted the large needle into Lucy's arm, she quivered with brief pain, but remained unconscious. Holmwood winced perceptibly at that, and again when his own arm was stabbed. Then he sat back quietly in his chair, holding the needle and tube in place with his free hand as the professor directed him. Arthur's anxious gaze seldom strayed from Lucy's face.

As minutes passed, and the rubber tubes carried their warm liquid burden, with the physicians now and then exchanging terse syllables of jargon regarding the transfusion's progress, something like life began to come back to Lucy's cheeks. The improvement was tentative and delicate at first, then more robust.

When he had observed this result until the reality of it could not be doubted, Van Helsing seemed to relax a little.

Presently, leaving the immediate supervision of the operation to Seward, the old man rummaged in his medical bag again, this time bringing out something Seward would have thought much less likely even than transfusion equipment: Van Helsing's hand emerged from the bag with a great handful of white flowers.

These, to the wonder of Seward and Holmwood, he arranged in a vase at Lucy's bedside, casually discarding the ordinary garden blooms already there. When that was done, more white flowers of the same type, already woven into a kind of loop, came out of the bag to be placed as a necklace over the patient's head. For these floral arrangements Van Helsing offered no explanation.

Seward avoided Holmwood's questioning eyes. He sniffed at the spreading odor of the white blooms, and tried to keep his own bewilderment from showing in his face.

Garlic?

Had he not known the old man so well for such a long time, young Dr. Seward would probably have judged him mad.

Evidently now satisfied with the decoration of the room, Van Helsing looked at his watch and replaced it in his pocket, then checked the condition of both recipient and donor and looked at his watch again. All three men could hear its ticking in the otherwise silent room.

At last the professor removed the tubes from the arms of both Arthur and Lucy and lightly dressed their wounded arms.

A few minutes later, Holmwood, though still looking a trifle pale, was on his feet again and putting on his coat when, without warning, Lucy's thin body was racked by a loud and raucous scream. It was a terrifying sound that for a moment made all three men recoil involuntarily from the bed.

Lucy shrieked again. "Is this why I cannot breathe?" With a surge of unnatural-seeming energy, she sat up in bed and hurled

ABOVE: In the year 1462, the mighty warrior Prince Dracula (Gary Oldman) returns from a battle defending the Christian faith.

RIGHT: Dracula finds his beautiful wife dead in the chapel.

Four hundred years later, Jonathan Harker (Keanu Reeves) is a guest at Dracula's castle in Transylvania.

The three female vampires who want to make Jonathan Harker a permanent resident of the castle.

Jonathan tries to escape from his terrifying prison.

Dr. Jack Seward (Richard E. Grant) and Professor Van Helsing (Anthony Hopkins) examine Lucy (Sadie Frost), who is beginning a frightening transformation.

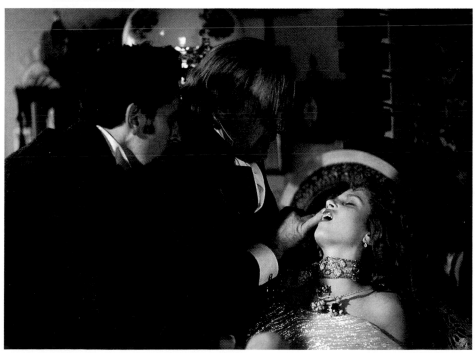

RIGHT: Winona Ryder as Mina.

BELOW: Van Helsing uses his cross to ward off Lucy, now a blood-thirsty vampire.

Dracula begins his seduction of innocent Mina.

Anthony Hopkins as Professor Van Helsing.

ABOVE: The burning of
Carfax Abbey.

RIGHT: The ancient Count Dracula
at his most malevolent.

Quincey Morris (Bill Campbell) in a fight to the death with Dracula.

Mina watches over Dracula's bloody corpse.

Director Francis Ford Coppola explains a scene to actress Winona Ryder.

the vase of white flowers from the nearby table to shatter on a distant patch of floor.

Van Helsing, for some reason, did not seem terribly surprised at this reaction. He said to the patient almost calmly: "The flowers are medicinal—so that you may sleep well—and dream pleasant—"

Laughing derisively, the girl in the bed violently tore off her necklace of blooms. "These flowers are common *garlic!*" Then she slumped back, her burst of energy exhausted.

After escorting Holmwood out of the room, Van Helsing and Seward returned to examine Lucy, who was now sleeping. At least, thought Seward, she appeared to be in substantially better condition than when Van Helsing had arrived.

The older man took care to point out to his younger colleague the pair of small, white-rimmed red punctures on the patient's throat.

"What do you make of these?" he asked his former student, squinting at him shrewdly.

Seward gave a weary shrug. "Mina—that's Miss Murray, Lucy's friend—has told me those wounds are the result of an unfortunate accident, with a safety pin, when Lucy was sleepwalking. It is true, they are very slow to heal."

From the way the professor was looking at him, Seward knew that he had given the wrong answer.

Drs. Seward and Van Helsing rejoined Holmwood in the hall. One of Lucy's maids, worried about her mistress, had gone in to sit with her for a while.

Following his ordeal, Holmwood naturally looked somewhat pale and dazed from loss of blood; and Van Helsing, speaking as if his mind were really elsewhere, advised the donor to eat heartily and get plenty of rest.

Then, halfway down the hallway, the old professor muttered, more to himself than to his companions: "The first gain is ours—but I fear for her still." And he threw a frowning glance over his shoulder in the direction of Lucy's room.

Arthur followed the pair of physicians. "My blood—did not cure her?"

Van Helsing, just reaching the head of the stairs and starting down, did not even turn his head but only laughed, somewhat bitterly, as if to himself.

Holmwood appealed silently to Seward for some explanation, but the look he received in return indicated a helplessness almost as profound as his own.

The three men continued out of the house into the formal garden, where on a happier day, about four months ago, Jonathan Harker had once waited to see his beloved Mina.

Now it was a warmly pleasant September night, for once not raining, inviting deep breathing and the contemplation of the stars. A gaslight, burning above the terrace, attracted moths and threw warm illumination on hedges and brickwork, on late-summer flowers and a small burbling fountain.

Holmwood, who before coming outdoors had detoured past the sideboard in the dining room, was now carrying a substantial amount of brandy in a snifter and fortifying himself with an occasional sip.

Van Helsing had said nothing for a little while. Now he finished lighting a cigar, threw away the match, then turned to challenge his younger colleague. "So? Can you tell me now why is this young lady bloodless?"

Seward could come up with no ready answer.

"Use your logic," Van Helsing urged him. "Think, man!"

Seward gazed up the broad flight of stairs leading to the terrace just outside Lucy's room, in which a dim light still burned. He mused: "There are those marks on her throat. Perhaps they were caused by something more than an accident with a pin, as Mina thought—possibly her major blood loss occurred there?"

Van Helsing made little meditative, grunting noises, seeming to express a qualified approval. His attitude seemed to indicate that his student was on the right track, but had not gone nearly far enough.

He said: "You were a careful student, Jack. Now you are master—or should be. Where did the blood go, Jack, eh? Come come—"

The younger doctor let out breath with a sigh. He shook his head at his own slow-wittedness. "How foolish of me! Not from those or any other external wounds. The bedclothes would be covered in blood." He paused.

"Yes? So?"

"Unless . . ." Seward hesitated again. A horrible explanation had seemed to shimmer in the air before him like a will-o'-the-wisp, only to be gone again before his mind could grasp it solidly.

The professor, now hovering close to Seward like the figure of some tempter in a play, was almost murmuring into his ear.

"Unless? Unless? So—so?"

Holmwood, meanwhile, could do no more than look on and listen in pitiable confusion.

Seward extended his hands, as if he might physically grope his way toward the truth, a truth still tantalizingly out of reach.

Van Helsing, chewing his cigar, relentlessly stalked him. "Hah—imagine, Jack, that you have a brain. Open it up. Show me what you are thinking now!"

Seward, in his frustration and anger, at last turned on the older physician, gesturing wildly. "Then all I can think of is that something has drained her life! I suppose something just went up there, sucked out her blood, and flew away?"

"*Ja.*" The answer was a flat, uncompromising challenge. "*Ja,* why not?"

"That's quite enough," said Holmwood firmly, and hiccuped. He had swallowed the last drops of brandy from his snifter, and in his debilitated state after the transfusion, the result was intoxication. He sat down shakily on a stone bench, letting the glass fall to the ground beside him.

The other two ignored him for the time being. Van Helsing still pursued his former student.

"Hear me out! Jack, you are a scientist. Do you not think there are things in this universe which you cannot understand—and yet which are true?" He gestured to the starry night above.

"You know I do not," Seward responded grimly.

His mentor was relentless. "Oh? Mesmerism? Hypnotism? Electromagnetic fields?"

The young man wearily conceded one point. "You and Charcot have proved hypnotism."

"Astral bodies? Materialization?"

"I don't know—"

"Aha! Just so . . . now you have admit that there is much you do not know, I tell you this—" And Van Helsing paused; making sure he had the total attention of both men. "Listen to me! There *is* a thing that drains her blood, as you have said. And dear Lucy, God help us, suckles from this *thing* its own diseased blood, with the result that she transform, to become what it is . . . a monster . . . a beast."

His listeners were speechless with horror; worse, with a lack of comprehension.

Morning had come again to England, and Mina was disturbed by hints she had heard from the servants of turmoil and illness in the house during the night. Following her late return from her strange encounter with the prince, she herself had retired to her room next to Lucy's, where she had fallen quickly into a deathlike oblivion of sleep and heard nothing.

To Mina's relief, she found Lucy this morning sleeping peacefully in her bedroom. The visitor, seeking anxiously for signs of improvement in her friend, had to admit that the pale face on the pillows looked only marginally better than it had yesterday.

Yesterday . . . how very long ago that seemed.

She, Mina, though technically her virginity was still preserved, was the one who now had an illicit lover. How strange, how incomprehensible!

And she knew, with a helpless, wonderful certainty, that she was going to see her prince again, as soon as possible.

11

Today Mina, seeking anonymity, had taken the train into town. She had gone to meet her prince, at his request, at Rule's Café later, a popular West End place, where, a few years earlier, the notorious poet Oscar Wilde might have been observed charming ladies and cultivating handsome young men.

Though lords and princes were common enough at Rule's, the imperious manner of Mina's escort, and a well-calculated donation of his money, promptly obtained for them a private dining room.

Food and wine were now on the table, and a violin was playing somewhere in the background—music lighthearted and sad by turns, that to Mina suggested Gypsies. The silhouettes of dancing couples were visible through the small room's walls of frosted glass.

The prince was saying to her: "The land of my forefathers is every bit as rich as is your England, in culture and fable and lore."

"Yes . . ." A fanciful scene of unaccustomed vividness was drifting through Mina's imagination. "I am willing to believe that it must be."

Her companion's eyes, startlingly blue with the dark glasses gone, twinkled as he smiled. "In my opinion, my homeland is the most beautiful place in all creation."

"Transylvania." Mina's voice, her mood, were absent, dreamy, almost giddy. She was sipping from a glass of milky-green absinthe, the drug of the moment for London café society, ordered in a moment's inexplicable impulse that was at least in keeping with the rest of her mad behavior this afternoon—or was it her companion who had suggested absinthe? At the moment she could not recall. But in her more lucid moments of this hour she thought the drink must be at least partially responsible for her condition.

Transylvania . . . dimly she could remember, months ago, Jonathan's voice speaking that same name . . . *some nobleman, in the exotic wilds of Transylvania* . . . yes, that was it. The same place, or near the place, where Jonathan was going, had gone, on business. His last letter, written so long ago, had come from somewhere in the region of Transylvania, from Castle Dracula. . . .

But the image of her fiancé faded swiftly.

She mused: "I see the meaning of the name . . . a land beyond a great, vast forest. Surrounded by mountains that are so majestic. And lush vineyards. And flowers, I can almost see them, inhale their fragrance; flowers of such frailty and beauty as can be found nowhere else on God's green earth."

The prince leaned forward. How young he is, she thought, watching the candlelight on his smooth face. How beautiful. Quite unlike all other men. Definitely superior to any of them.

He said quietly: "You describe my home as if you might already have seen it at first hand."

Mina allowed her eyes to close—for just a moment. The closing was so restful. From the darkness behind her lids she said: "It is your voice, perhaps. So . . . *familiar* . . . like a voice in a dream that you cannot place. It comforts me . . . when I am alone."

Her eyes came open again; so easily, yet sleepily. She met the gaze of her companion, and Mina was distantly aware that the contact was far too prolonged. Then suddenly, just how she was not sure, he had come to be seated close beside her. His right hand was at her throat, fingers gently but firmly tracing, caressing. Quite possessively, as if this were the most natural thing in all the world . . .

Suddenly a giddy laugh burst from her lips. Something made her get to her feet, breaking the physical contact, as if she knew this was the last chance she would ever have to do so . . . then out of nowhere a question came to her lips.

"And what of the princess?"

That made his blue eyes blink. "Princess?"

Mina looked out into the main room of the café. "It seems to me there must be always a princess. With flowing hair the color of . . . of . . . and the haunting eyes of a lustful cat. Long gowns, in a style that is—very old. Her face a . . . ."

Something like an hallucination was stealing over Mina. This was more than merely vivid imagination. She knew that she was still here, in London, in Rule's Café, and yet . . . another reality was also present.

". . . a river," Mina said clearly. "The princess is in a river—no, she *is* a river, all filled with tears of sadness, heartbreak. . . ."

And then the spell, or whatever it had been, was gone. Not gone, but weakened sufficiently for Mina to see what a powerful effect her words had had upon the prince.

Raising her hands to her face, she said: "I must sound terribly foolish. The absinthe . . . I shouldn't drink it. You think me ridiculous."

"Never that, Elisabeth. Never that. You see, there was a princess."

"You must tell me about her."

"I shall."

And he was standing, holding out his hand in an invitation to the dance. The violin was singing somewhere, and the absinthe sang in Mina's brain as she arose, only to be swirled away into a graceful waltz, among what seemed a thousand candles. . . .

The mood of dreamlike exaltation lasted until early the next morning, when Mina, seated alone upon her favorite garden bench at Hillingham, counting the minutes till she might see her prince again, looked up to see an eager Hobbs approaching. In the butler's hand a silver salver bore what could only be a letter. All the servants knew how desperately their young guest had been waiting for a certain message.

Trembling, Mina inspected the envelope; certainly not Jonathan's writing, but coming from Budapest, it must bear news of him. With shaking fingers Mina ripped the message open. It was from Sister Agatha, of the Hospital of St. Joseph and Ste. Mary.

> Dear Madam—
> I write by desire of Mr. Jonathan Harker, who is himself not strong enough to write, though progressing well, thanks to God and St. Joseph and Ste. Mary. He has been under our care for nearly six weeks, suffering from a violent brain fever. He wishes me to convey his love. . . .

Jonathan was alive. He was alive! Leaping to her feet, ignoring Hobbs's murmured congratulations on the good news, Mina began to run through the garden, beside herself with joy, eager to share her happiness. . . . but before she had run more than a few steps, her steps abruptly slowed.

How could she have forgotten, even for a moment, the one who in the past few days had come to be the center of her life?

"My sweet prince," she murmured, almost inaudibly. "Jonathan must never know of us."

In a moment her purposeful movement toward the house had resumed, though at a slower pace. There was no question but that she must go to Jonathan at once.

Climbing the steps briskly, approaching Lucy's room, Mina encountered Dr. Seward on the terrace. He was deep in conversation with an older, distinguished-looking man she had never met.

The latter turned, regarded her with a pair of penetrating blue eyes, and with a small and almost military bow, succinctly introduced himself.

"Abraham Van Helsing."

Mina was already thinking that this could hardly be anyone but Lucy's latest doctor, of whom she had often heard Jack Seward speak.

The professor continued: "And you are Miss Mina Murray, dear friend to our Lucy."

"How is she, Doctor?"

"Still very weak. She tells of your beloved Jonathan Harker and your worry for him . . . but today you have perhaps good news?"

"Yes, very good . . . a letter . . ." Here it was, still in her hand.

"That is excellent. I worry, too, for all young lovers." To Mina's surprise, the good doctor suddenly began to sing, and before she understood exactly what was happening or why, his arm—that of a gentlemanly dancing partner—had gone around her, and the two of them were waltzing on the terrace, under the bemused gaze of Jack Seward.

Abruptly the dance was over. Van Helsing, with something mesmeric in his eyes, was gazing directly into Mina's. Softly he said: "There are darknesses in life, and there are lights. You are one of the lights, dear Mina. Go now, see your friend."

Moments later, sitting down beside the bed in Lucy's room, Mina took hold of the poor wasted hand. There was good news to relate, news that at least to its bearer seemed important enough to justify waking the patient.

Somewhere a door, escaping from some servant's careless hand, banged shut. Outside in the great curve of drive, a horse's hooves scuffed gravel. Presently Lucy stirred. Her eyes opened slowly, then focused with some difficulty.

Her voice was soft and tentative. "Mina, dearest . . . where have you been?"

"You're freezing cold, Luce." Mina, distracted from her own good news by Lucy's sad condition, gently rubbed the cold hand she was holding, trying thus to encourage life.

Lucy pulled herself up a little in the bed and summoned up a trace of her old coquettishness.

"And you're so warm. Did you know, dear, Jack Seward has been playing doctor with me?"

"I know."

"Did you meet him? I've told him all about you."

"Yes, I met Dr. Seward, Lucy. At the party, weeks and weeks ago, remember?" Mina reached to pull an untouched food tray closer on the bedside table. "He's a doctor for lunatics, and you are not a lunatic. What you need is proper care. Now eat your porridge, Goldilocks."

Weakly Lucy turned her head away, rejecting the spoon as if its contents were disgusting. She whispered: "I'm too fat. Arthur loathes me fat."

Mina felt a chill as she contrasted those words with the fact of the almost cadaverous form before her. Gently but firmly, as if dealing with a baby, she got a spoonful of oatmeal into Lucy's mouth.

The girl made a face, but swallowed. Then she squinted questioningly at her caretaker.

"What is it, Mina? You actually look happy for a change."

Mina flushed slightly.

Lucy managed to produce a smile. "You've heard from Jonathan. Is that it?"

Mina nodded. Now her good news came pouring out in a rush. "Not exactly from him, but yes, he's safe. He's been six weeks—longer, now—in a hospital in Budapest. A letter came just now from one of the good sisters who are caring for him. They say he needs me badly, and I must go to him at once—but I do so hate to leave you like this—"

Making a great effort, Lucy pushed herself further up in the bed to hug Mina with failing arms. Softly she murmured in Mina's ear: "Mina—go to him. Love him, and marry him, right then and there. Don't waste another precious moment of life without each other."

Exhausted, Lucy fell back on her pillows. The two girls stared at each other in silence for a long moment, seeming to exchange important confidences without the need for speech.

Then Lucy pulled off her engagement ring. The diamonded gold slid easily from her wasted finger.

She held it out to her friend. "Take this, sister. . . . Let it be my wedding gift to you—and Jonathan. Take it. . . ."

Mina, overwhelmed and unable to speak, kept shaking her head, trying to refuse.

"Bad luck if you say no." Lucy's voice had fallen back into a terrible whisper. Her strength was obviously failing.

Again she rallied, briefly. "Tell Jonathan . . . oceans of love from me . . . millions of kisses. . . ."

On the evening of the day of Mina's departure Dracula, sitting impatient and alone in the private dining room at Rule's Café, his sensitive hearing tuned to every opening of the street door of the restaurant, was brought a note by a waiter.

As he accepted the paper a shadow crossed the youthful face of the elegantly dressed man; he had not for a moment really expected that the woman he loved (and who, he knew, loved him, despite all her formal protestations about a fiancé) would temporize, play coy, and quibble about coming to him again. But perhaps some truly unavoidable circumstance had arisen—

Tipping the waiter with a common coin, he tore open the envelope to discover that as he had expected, it came from Mina. It was the content of the message that brought total shock.

My dearest Prince, forgive me, but I cannot be with you now or any other time. I have received word from my fiancé in Budapest. I am on my way to join him. We are to be married.

Forever your love, Mina.

Convulsively the prince's hand crumpled the note. All thoughts of love and tenderness were gone, wiped out in an instant, in a collision with a red wall of rage and injury.

He could hear himself, and others outside his room of privacy could hear him, breathing with the sounds of a wounded animal.

The note had not been delivered until well past midnight, and by then Mina was almost a full day along on her trip by train to Budapest. She was following the route taken months ago by her beloved Jonathan; from London, via Dover, to Paris, and thence eastward.

Once more she opened and reread the letter from Budapest, concentrating now upon its closing sentences.

P.S. My patient being asleep, I open this to let you know something more. He has told me all about you, and that you are shortly to be his wife. All blessings to you both! He has had some fearful shock— so says our doctor—and in his delirium his ravings have been dreadful; of wolves and poison and blood; of ghosts and demons; and I fear to say of what. Be careful of him always that there may be nothing of this kind to excite him for a long time to come; the traces of an illness such as his do not lightly die away. We should have written long ago, but we knew nothing of his friends. He came in the train from Klausenburg, and the guard was told by the stationmaster there that he rushed into the station shouting for a ticket for home. Seeing from his violent demeanor that he was English, they gave him a ticket for the farthest station on the way thither that the train reached.

Be assured that he is well cared for. He is truly getting on well, and I have no doubt in a few weeks will be all himself. But be careful of him for safety's sake. There are, I pray God and St. Joseph and Ste. Mary, many, many happy years for you both.

While Mina Murray rode ever farther into the east, at Hillingham the bitter struggle went on, day after day, night after night. There were afternoon hours when Lucy seemed on the road to recovery, times in the morning when she appeared to linger at the point of death. One day Mrs. Westenra, tottering in to see her daughter when the doctors were absent, was offended by the rank smell of garlic and ordered Van Helsing's daily crop of small white garlic flowers thrown away; a loss that caused the professor great consternation when he discovered it.

Three days after the first transfusion of blood, another became necessary; this time Dr. Seward was the donor. Taking his turn in the chair at Lucy's bedside, he thought that no man could know, until he experienced it, what it was to feel his own lifeblood drawn away into the veins of the woman he loved.

And in another three days, a fresh deterioration in the condition of the patient required a third transfusion, this time from Van Helsing's veins.

And almost a week after that, on Sunday, the eighteenth of September, when Arthur Holmwood was in attendance at his father's deathbed, the operation was yet once more repeated, and Quincey Morris became the fourth man to contribute blood to Lucy.

On the night of the next day the Texan, a trifle pale but maintaining that he had regained sufficient strength for any kind of action, was cradling a Winchester rifle in his arms as he walked beside Jack Seward down the stair into the great hall of Hillingham.

Quincey was saying to his old hunting comrade: "Jack, you know I love that girl same as you."

"I have no doubt of it, old fellow."

"That ol' Dutchman really know what he's doin'? How much blood have we given her, and where's it all goin'?"

Seward shook his head wearily. "I learned years ago that I'm not wise enough to question Van Helsing's methods. . . . Frankly, Quincey, I'm at my wit's end."

Quincey rubbed his arm, still sore from the professor's needle. "Well, he could outspook a Borneo witch doctor, if ya ask me. Know what this reminds me of? I had a fine mare down in the pampas once, and one of those big bats they call vampires got at her in the night. What with the bat feeding and the vein left open, there wasn't enough blood in her to let her stand up, and I had to shoot her. Damn fine animal."

Van Helsing, putting on his coat in preparation to go out, joined the two men at the front door. If he had heard Quincey's comments, he gave no sign of any reaction to them.

The old doctor said: "Jack, hurry, man, I have much to tell you—and important things I must learn for myself tonight." He shifted his gaze to the other. "Guard her well, Mr. Morris!"

"Reckon I will." Quincey's tone and manner made it plain that he did not care much for this old man.

Van Helsing laughed, oblivious to what the Texan thought of him. The professor, despite the setbacks and the protracted struggle, was still caught up in the joy of battle, the elation of discovery.

"If we fail, your precious Lucy becomes the devil's whore. I advise you, rely more on the garlic and the crucifix than on your rifle."

Quincey, now ready to punch the old man out, moved forward half a step. "You're a sick old buzzard—"

Van Helsing sobered. "And I suppose that you are sane men, both of you. If so, hear me out! The truth, as I have tried repeatedly to tell you, is that Lucy invites the beast into her bedchamber! She suckles the beast's own diseased blood, and it must transform her, make her what *it* is!"

The Texan, feeling helpless, taken aback by the earnest intensity with which the old man made this monstrous assertion, looked to Seward for counsel, but got none.

Van Helsing laughed again, a sound containing more than a touch of hysteria, while the two younger men now stared at him as if both of them were paralyzed.

"Into the coach, Jack," his mentor ordered, recovering from his emotional fit. "We must talk. And I must go where I can learn. What we have done for our young Miss Lucy so far is not enough."

"Where is that, sir—where you can learn?"

"I have had word from an old friend. In the British Museum there is a room where he will allow me entrance, where certain secrets may be made known to me, if I know where to look. I do not want to waste an hour. We go now!"

Arthur Holmwood's father still clung to life, in another sickbed in another house, at Ring. Meanwhile, tonight, Arthur was watching at the bedside of his beloved Lucy. Aware of Van Helsing's warnings, though far from understanding them, Holmwood kept his vigil with a brace of loaded pistols handy on the table, beside the vase holding the old professor's daily crop of garlic flowers.

But on Arthur the long days of futile struggle against he knew not what, of bitter grief as both his father and the woman he loved lingered at the point of death, had taken their inevitable toll. He was having trouble staying awake.

And now, even as Arthur dozed off, Lucy suddenly awakened. The young woman's eyes were open in an instant, and she experienced a surge of joy and demonic energy. She scarcely glanced at the figure of her fiancé nodding beside her bed. But she still lay quietly—because she knew—knew with a deep, unholy happiness— that there was no need to move.

Her vampire lover was approaching, and *he* would certainly find her, as he had so many times before. No watch set by ordinary men, no barriers they might put up, no scheme they might devise, could keep him out.

Quincey Morris had at last been persuaded by the old man's repeated references to a bloodsucking beast. It was for this reason that the Texan tonight had taken up his lonely, self-appointed vigil on the grounds. Quincey—most often with Seward and Holmwood as his companions—had hunted large predators from Sumatra to Siberia, and it was a game he well understood.

Or so he had thought.

It was a quiet night, though a trifle windy now—no sign of any intruders on the grounds. Of course there never was. And yet, no matter what kind of defenses were arranged, it seemed that the enemy—if there was a real, predatory enemy, and Van Helsing was not a lunatic—somehow, one way or another, got through.

Quincey, lost in contemplation of the seemingly unresolvable problem, was yet alerted by his keen hearing, or by some hunter's instinct. He turned, in time to glimpse the onrushing presence of a shadowy, inhuman figure. In the next instant he had snapped up his rifle and fired at it—accurately, his instinct told him, yet without effect.

In the next moment Quincey Morris had been knocked down, and knocked out, by some superhuman embodiment of force that rushed on past him in the direction of the house.

The leaping form of a wolf came smashing straight in through the glass of Lucy's French window. The shock and noise of crashing glass instantly brought Holmwood wide-awake in his bedside chair; but Arthur's awakening came too late, and in any case he was ill prepared to take any effective action. In a moment he had been hurled aside by the same force that had struck down Quincey, and crumpled unconscious in a corner of the room.

In the next instant the great gray beast shape, slavering, leaped upon the bed, where Lucy, laughing, crooning, fiercely rejoicing, welcomed it with open arms.

Gripping the short fur of the huge head in both her hands, she pulled the wolf fangs hungrily against her body. . . .

* * *

It was at almost the same moment that a carriage pulled to a stop in Great Russell Street, near the middle of London. In a moment the vehicle had discharged two passengers before the British Museum, the huge bulk of the building at this hour almost entirely dark.

Late on the previous evening, as usual, the endless book stacks of the reading room had been closed to ordinary visitors. But now, in the small hours of the morning, one of the museum's elderly senior curators was soon guiding a pair of urgent seekers after knowledge through part of the vast building: one visitor was the curator's old friend Abraham Van Helsing, and the second was the worried Dr. Seward.

The destination sought by the three men was a small and very private reading room, whose unmarked door the curator had to unlock with a private key to allow them access.

The door of the comparatively small room creaked in on rusty hinges. At once Van Helsing, muttering under his breath, plunged in urgently among the tall dusty stacks and shelves, immersing himself in the smell of old paper and old wood, while the curator muttered words of guidance, and Seward held a pair of lamps.

The professor was soon elated to discover the very book he had come looking for.

It was an old and heavy volume, fastened with a locked clasp, which the curator had to produce another key to open.

Eagerly Van Helsing blew dust from his find, then propped it on a reading stand and began turning the stiff pages. The bulk of the printed text, he saw without surprise, was in German, the rest in other languages from farther east, tongues far less commonly understood in London. But most of them the professor could read, at least sufficiently to guide him in his search.

With Seward anxiously hanging over his shoulder, continuing to hold a lamp where it would be most useful, Van Helsing read, tracing lines of text with his finger, muttering to himself, translating scraps of information aloud into English.

"Here begins the frightening and shocking story of the wild berserker Prince Dracula. How he impaled people and roasted them and boiled their heads in a kettle and skinned people and hacked them to pieces and drank their blood."

Grim satisfaction grew in the old man. What he was reading

confirmed what he had all along suspected. It gave him a better grip upon the fantastic and yet sobering truth.

But neither of the physicians realized that the knowledge they were gaining came too late to do their patient any good.

That battle was already lost.

12

$\mathbf{S}$unrise had come to Hillingham, on the morning after the final monstrous assault on Lucy. Everyone in the house—except perhaps Mrs. Westenra, from whom the bitter defeat was still concealed—knew by now that the long, agonizing weeks of struggle for the young woman's life were finally drawing to their grim conclusion. The ugly truth seemed to hang in the air, though no one voiced it openly, and almost no one had any real understanding of its nature.

Among those who had fought to save the girl, only one man, Van Helsing, had any real comprehension of the horror that menaced her. And for him that knowledge was very hard to act upon successfully, not least because it was almost impossible to communicate to others. How, without himself being confined as a madman, to convince the skeptical moderns of these last years of the enlightened nineteenth century? Indeed, there were hours when the professor almost despaired of ever being able to convey the truth.

Quincey Morris had suffered no serious injury from his mysterious assailant. On recovering his wits to find himself sprawled on the dewy lawn, a trifle bruised but otherwise unharmed, the Texan had become an enthusiastic convert to Van Helsing's announced view that a great beast of some kind must be responsible for Lucy's condition—a beast that was somehow devilishly immune to Winchesters. On that point Morris now stood ready to offer personal testimony.

To no one's surprise, Arthur Holmwood's father, Lord Godalming, had passed away during the night, in his ancestral home at Ring. Very early this morning Arthur had received the news by special messenger. Now, struggling to cope with his father's death—long expected but no lighter a burden for that—Arthur was trying to catch some sleep on a sofa in a room near Lucy's.

At a little before six in the morning, Van Helsing came in to relieve his younger colleague, and bent over the patient for a close examination.

As soon as the old man got a close look at Lucy's face, Seward could hear the hissing intake of his breath.

"Draw up the blind," the professor commanded. "I want light!"

Seward hastened to comply.

Van Helsing now removed the garlic flowers, and a silk handkerchief Lucy had been wearing about her throat.

"The devil's whore!" he murmured, in a despairing tone.

Seward hastened to look for himself, and as he did a queer chill came over him.

The wounds on the throat had absolutely disappeared.

For fully five minutes Van Helsing stood looking at the young patient, with his face at its sternest. Then he turned to Seward and said calmly: "She is dying; it will not be long now. Wake that poor boy, and let him come see the last. He trusts us, and we have promised him."

Seward accordingly went to the nearby room where Holmwood was and awakened him, assuring Arthur that Lucy was still asleep, but conveying as gently as he could the opinion of both doctors that the end was near.

When the two returned to Lucy's room, Seward noted that Van Helsing had been putting matters straight and making everything look as pleasant as possible. He had even brushed Lucy's hair, so that it lay on the pillow in its usual bright ripples.

When Holmwood came into the room, she opened her eyes and, seeing her fiancé, whispered softly: "Arthur! Oh, my love, I am so glad you have come!"

He was stooping to kiss her when Van Helsing motioned him back. "No, not yet. Hold her hand. It will comfort her more."

So Arthur, after giving the old man a questioning look, obediently took Lucy's hand and knelt beside her, and she looked her best, with all the soft lines matching the angelic beauty of her eyes.

Then gradually her eyes closed, and she sank to sleep. For a little bit her breast heaved softly, and her breath came and went like that of a tired child.

And then, insensibly at first, there followed the strange change that Seward had noticed before. Her breathing grew stertorous, the mouth opened, and the pale gums, somewhat drawn back, made the teeth look longer and sharper than ever.

In a sort of sleepwalking, vague, unconscious way Lucy opened her eyes, which Seward now perceived as being both dull and hard at once. She said again in a soft, voluptuous voice: "Arthur! Oh, my love, I am so glad you have come! Kiss me!"

This time Arthur bent eagerly over the woman he loved to kiss her; but at that instant Van Helsing, who, like Seward, had been startled by her changed voice, swooped upon him, and catching him by the neck with both hands, dragged him back with furious strength and actually hurled him almost across the room.

"Not for your life!" he said. "Not for your living soul and hers!" And he stood between the couple like a lion at bay.

Arthur was so taken aback that he did not for a moment know what to do or say; and before any impulse of violence could seize him, he realized the place and the occasion, and stood silent, waiting.

Lucy at first snarled—there was no other word for it, thought Seward—at Van Helsing when he intervened so forcefully, but a minute later, in a last softening of her appearance and her manner, she blessed and thanked him.

"My true friend!" she said in a faint voice, pressing Van Helsing's hand hard with her wasted fingers. "My true friend, and his. Oh, guard him, and give me peace."

Van Helsing dropped solemnly to one knee beside her bed. "I swear it!"

And then Lucy's breathing became stertorous again, and all at once it ceased.

Shortly after sunrise, with Arthur Holmwood numbly still in attendance, Dr. Seward pronounced the patient dead, and within the hour had signed her death certificate.

By noon, Lucy, looking pure and lovely, lay peacefully on white satin in her glassy funeral coffin, in the great hall, surrounded by masses of lilies and roses.

Every hour, Seward mused privately, gazing at the figure under glass, seemed to be enhancing Lucy's loveliness. It frightened and amazed him somewhat, and he was not surprised that Arthur should tremble, and finally be shaken with real doubt.

There came a moment when Holmwood leaned toward him and asked in a faint whisper: "Jack, is she really dead?"

The physician had to assure his friend that it was so.

Meanwhile Lucy's invalid mother had collapsed upon being told the news; there was no way the bitter truth could be any longer kept from her. Mrs. Westenra was being attended to by her maids, and by her own physician, in her own room. Seward expected to hear at any moment that the mother had followed her daughter.

In the early afternoon, Holmwood and Quincey Morris, both near tears and unable to sleep, were sitting a vigil near the head of Lucy's coffin.

Van Helsing and Seward, both grief-stricken also, had been conferring at a little distance. Now, after Van Helsing signaled Seward with a look, the two physicians turned away and walked into the conservatory, where it would be possible to hold a more private conversation.

The elder man said: "I know you loved her deeply. What I discovered last night came too late to save her life." He paused. "But there is worse still to be feared."

Seward could feel his own face twitching; he could only stare at his old mentor aghast. "Worse! In God's name, Professor, what could be worse than what we have endured?"

"Jack, will you trust me?"

"To do what?"

If Van Helsing was bothered by the new lack of unqualified trust, he did not comment. His gaze had become remote; his mind was busy planning out his own agenda.

His voice, when he spoke again, was calm. "I want you to bring me, today or tomorrow, a set of postmortem knives."

"Then must we make an autopsy?" Seward's tone was almost despairing.

"Yes, and no. I want to operate, but not as you think. Let me tell you now, but not a word to another." The philosopher's voice was chillingly matter-of-fact. "I want to cut off her head and take out her heart."

Seward uttered a wordless gasp.

"Ah, you a surgeon, and so shocked—but I must not forget, my dear friend John, that you loved her."

"I did indeed."

"Still, you must help me. . . . I would like to do it tonight, but for Arthur's sake I must not; he will be free after his father's funeral tomorrow, and he will want to see his beloved again before interment.

"Then later, when she is coffined, whether in the vault or not, you and I shall come some night when all are asleep. We shall unscrew the coffin lid, and do our operation, and then replace all so that none know, save we alone."

Seward had recovered somewhat from his shock, but was still depressed and puzzled. "But why do it at all, Professor? The poor girl is dead—why this mutilation? I see nothing to gain, no good to her, to us, to science, to human knowledge . . . ?"

Van Helsing's attitude became one of great fatherly tenderness. "Friend John, I pity your poor bleeding heart. There are things you know not, but shall know—though they are not pleasant things.

"Were you not amazed, nay horrified, when I would not let Arthur kiss his love—though she was dying—and snatched him away by all my strength?"

"Frankly I was."

"Yes! And yet you saw how she thanked me, with her so beautiful dying eyes, and she kiss my rough old hand and bless me?" Van Helsing held up the hand Lucy had kissed, and Seward saw that it was trembling slightly.

"Yes, I did see that."

The professor continued: "And did you not hear me swear promise to her, so that she closed her eyes grateful?"

"Yes, I saw and heard all that as well."

"Well, I have good reason now for all I want to do. Trust me, Jack. The best of reasons."

Mrs. Westenra, as expected, survived by no more than a few hours the shock of the death of her only child.

Seward wrote in his journal that in a double funeral the old lady had been laid to rest, beside her daughter Lucy, "in the tomb of her kin, a lordly death house . . . away from teeming London, where the air is fresh, and the sun rises over Hampstead Hill, and where wildflowers grow of their own accord."

* * *

Just before dawn on the edge of Hampstead Heath, a homeless urchin, dressed in rags and no more than seven or eight years old, was warming his chapped hands and bare feet beside a small fire of wooden scraps and scavenged bits of coal.

The lad was distracted from his chronic hunger and discomfort, his attention very much engaged, by the sight of a young, pretty, red-haired woman walking toward him from the direction in which the sun was soon to rise. The lady was quite alone at the moment, dressed all in delicate and frilly white, so that her unsophisticated admirer wondered if she might be a bride. She smiled graciously at the small boy as he stared, openmouthed, at the passing vision of loveliness.

Watching the woman disappear out of sight on her effortless but swift passage in the general direction of Hillingham, he murmured to himself: "Coo . . . wot a bloofer lady, she is. . . ."

But moments later, looking back in the direction from which the apparition had come, the urchin caught sight of a motionless pair of legs no bigger than his own, protruding from some bushes.

Practical matters first. Approaching the apparently lifeless victim, the shivering child began to remove the shoes from the small feet, thinking that he himself had greater need of them. Whereupon the owner of the shoes stirred and sat up, crying feebly—it was another boy, perhaps a little younger than the first. His skin had been drained of color, and he was disoriented.

On his neck were a pair of tiny wounds, still fresh, each marked with a drop of blood.

Later that same day, Van Helsing, having been shocked by a newspaper account of this strange event, swore in German and muttered in Seward's hearing: "So soon! So soon!"

Taking the paper, Seward read:

THE WESTMINSTER GAZETTE, 25 SEPTEMBER

A HAMPSTEAD MYSTERY

We have just received intelligence that another child, missed last night, was discovered late in the morning under a furze bush at the Shooter's Hill side of Hampstead Heath, which is, perhaps, less frequented than the other parts. It has the same tiny wound in the throat as has been noticed in other cases. It was terribly weak, and looked quite emaciated. It, too, when partially restored, had the common story to tell of being lured away by the "bloofer lady."

Within the hour the professor, accompanied by Dr. Seward, was in the charity ward of the North Heath Hospital. There the two visiting physicians, having quickly established their credentials with the doctor in charge, were shown to the bedside of a small patient who had been recently admitted.

Van Helsing began by presenting a candy. Then, deftly lifting a bandage, he looked at the wounds on the childish throat, making sure that Seward got the chance to see them also.

Then the professor restored the bandage and sat back in his chair. "Now, lad—I need your help. Dr. Vincent tells me it is his idea that some animal bit you. Maybe it was a rat? Maybe a bat?"

The boy shook his head. "It was 'at bloofer lady."

"A lady who was beautiful, you say, if I have understanding—yes?"

A nod.

"Good. Well now, this lady's hair was—gray, perhaps? Or was it black?"

The small head shook from side to side. The sweet had already vanished into the small hungry mouth, and Van Helsing, when prodded by Seward, offered another.

Speaking around the candy clenched in his teeth, the young lad told them firmly: "No, sir, guv'nor. She got 'air all red. Bright. Like an angel. But she bit me, she did."

A few minutes later Seward and Van Helsing were walking out of the hospital.

"*Mein Gott!*" the old man was murmuring to himself again. "So soon, so soon!"

Seward cleared his throat, and stated the one point in the whole affair he had been able to grasp firmly. "The small puncture wounds were exactly like poor Lucy's. Presumably it is the same in the case of the other children also."

His mentor's eyes looked at him sideways from under their heavy brows. "Certainly they were alike. And what do you make of that?"

"Simply that there is some cause in common—the small holes

in the children's throats were made by the same agency that injured Lucy."

"Then you are wrong. Oh, would it were so! But alas, no. It is worse, far, far, worse."

Seward stopped in surprise, confronting his companion. "In God's name, Professor Van Helsing, what do you mean?"

The old man made a despairing gesture. "They were made by Miss Lucy!"

It was on that same day that Jonathan and Mina Harker returned to England as man and wife, having been married at the convent hospital in Budapest. An additional time of convalescence, and the presence and attentions of his loving bride, had now restored Harker, at least as far as outward appearances were concerned, to something approaching a normal state of health. A pallor and a limp, the latter assisted by a cane, were the most highly visible remaining signs of his ordeal.

The couple arrived at Dover by boat-train from France, then proceeded by another train to London.

At Dover they had been greeted by a telegram from Van Helsing, bringing them the news, sad but not unexpected, of the almost simultaneous deaths of Lucy and her mother.

The professor also requested the Harkers to get in touch with him as soon as possible in London, where he had taken a room at the Berkeley Hotel.

On reaching London, the Harkers disembarked from their train at Victoria Station. Since Jonathan was still on convalescent leave, with pay, from his employer, they decided that they might as well stay at the Berkeley themselves.

As the couple, with their modest baggage, boarded a hansom cab, Mina was musing, as much to herself as to her new husband: "I can't believe Lucy is gone . . . never to return to us. She was so full of life. How she must have suffered. Her life and mine were so different only a few months ago. All our hopes—our dreams—"

Harker, who had barely been acquainted with Lucy, commiserated with his wife, but meanwhile he was looking greedily out the window of the cab, drinking in the cheerfully strenuous life of London, rejoicing in his own successful return to the homelike sights and sounds of the metropolis, which, in recent months, he had more than once despaired of ever seeing again.

Amid the clamor, the ever-changing life of the familiar streets, he at last began truly to relax. This made the blow all the worse when, a few minutes later, with the hansom momentarily stalled in traffic, he got one of the worst shocks of his life.

He saw Dracula, unmistakably the Carpathian count, though now looking young and vital and dressed in modern Western garb. The figure of Dracula was standing under a street lamp and gazing arrogantly back at Harker in his cab.

Dracula, giving the impression that Harker's presence was no surprise at all, favored his former prisoner with a knowing look, then deliberately turned away and entered a pub.

Harker tried to leap to his feet, but his worn nerves failed him for the moment and his knees buckled.

Mina caught him, tried to cradle him, stared with alarm at her husband's eyes gone wild in terror and amazement.

"Jonathan? What is it?"

Harker pointed feverishly out the window as he stammered out his answer. "It—it is the man himself. The count. I s-saw him; he has grown young!"

Mina felt a cold chill at her heart. She looked out of the cab, which still had not moved, but whoever had so excited her husband had disappeared.

Harker was suddenly animated, his eyes and his voice once more lucid with purpose.

"Carfax!" he exclaimed, snapping his fingers. "The bastard's there."

"Carfax—the estate you sold him."

Harker nodded. "One of them. Yes." Hastily digging into his traveling bag, he pulled out a slim volume. It was the journal the young man had kept while a prisoner in Dracula's castle, and which he had somehow managed to carry with him during his escape.

Feverishly Harker pressed the book into Mina's hands.

He gazed at her pleadingly. "Up to now, my dear one, I have told you only the bare outline of events in that hellish place. Now I want you to read every word. You will understand . . . I pray you will. . . ."

Her hands closed on the slim volume. "What are you going to do, Jonathan?"

"What I must!" And in the next moment Harker had jumped

out of the cab and was moving, as swiftly as his cane and his limp would allow, in pursuit of Dracula.

Elbowing his way across the crowded pavement, Harker hurried into the pub, where he stood peering desperately through the smoky haze of the interior.

The traffic snarl was easing. Mina ordered the cabdriver to pull to the curb and wait, and when the man seemed disinclined to do so, she reinforced the command with a gift of coins.

Inside the pub, Harker caught sight of the man he sought at the last instant, just as Dracula was leaving the smoke-filled room by a different door. Once again forcing people out of his way, ignoring their protests, Harker followed.

Outside again, now in a foggy alley, he caught another tantalizing glimpse of the retreating count; a figure turning, smiling, almost beckoning to his pursuer.

Again Harker followed—for the moment rage and indignation were enough to overcome fear, and even common sense.

Suddenly the fog surrounding Harker was swirled by a whirlwind of force. The incredible figure of a bat, dark, gigantic, man-sized, exploded from the mist, hurling the man back.

Harker, falling hard on cobblestones and wall, was stunned.

13

In the depth of the September night, amid chill and fog, four men burdened with tools, weapons, and lanterns were stealthily entering the cemetery at Hillingham.

Van Helsing was of course the one who had instigated and organized this expedition, and he remained in charge, with Seward his tight-lipped and ill-informed assistant. The professor had chosen this dark hour in the hopes of avoiding observation by the servants and the potentially troublesome gossip that must inevitably follow.

Quincey Morris, as puzzled as ever about the exact nature of the enemy, but determined to stand by his friends, was walking beside the doubly bereaved Arthur Holmwood—who had now, upon the death of his father, inherited the title of Lord Godalming.

Both Quincey and Arthur were even more in the dark than Dr. Seward regarding the purpose of this foray, and both were coming along more or less reluctantly. Both had been horrified and mystified at Van Helsing's claim that some vitally important task must be accomplished in the Westenra family mausoleum tonight.

The four men stayed in a tight group as they left the house by a side door and entered the section of the grounds where the Westenra family were interred. Once they were inside the borders of the graveyard, passing the headstones of distant cousins and family retainers, Van Helsing led them straight toward the imposing aboveground entrance of the old family crypt.

According to Lucy's will, Arthur Holmwood had inherited all of the young woman's property, including that which had been her mother's; therefore Arthur was now armed with all the keys of the estate. Reluctantly, at an imperious signal from the old man and a confirming nod from Seward, Holmwood now opened the iron gates defending the vault in which for centuries members of the immediate family had been interred. The lock worked smoothly; it had been oiled for the double funeral only a few days ago.

Silently Van Helsing, who was carrying one of the lanterns, led his followers in, and down.

As he followed his mentor down the echoing stone stairs, Seward could remember with painful clarity how the tomb had looked in the daytime, at the burial of Lucy and her mother. Then the interior of the mausoleum, though wreathed with fresh flowers, had looked grim and gruesome enough. But now, in the light of the lanterns the men were carrying, the flowers were already beginning to hang lank and dead, their whites turning to rust and their greens to browns. Here the spider and the beetle had resumed their accustomed dominance; and time-discolored stone, and dust-encrusted mortar, and rusty, dank iron and tarnished brass, and clouded silver plating gave back the feeble glimmer of a candle. The effect, thought Seward, was more miserable and sordid than could have been imagined.

On reaching the vaulted underground mausoleum, Van Helsing went about his work systematically. Handing his lantern to another, he lighted a candle and held it so he could read the coffin plates. By these means he ascertained which coffin was Lucy's. It rested in a kind of sarcophagus, under a lid of heavy stone, which, at his direction, the men soon moved aside.

Holmwood cleared his throat, a startling sound in the chill silence. Abruptly he said: "Must we desecrate Lucy's grave? She died horribly enough—"

Van Helsing, having arranged several lights to his satisfaction, raised a hand. His manner was didactic, almost that of a professor lecturing. "If Miss Lucy is dead, we can do no wrong to her tonight. But, on the other hand, if she is not—"

At this suggestion Holmwood almost collapsed. "My God, what are you saying—has she been buried alive?"

The professor looked at him calmly enough. "I go no further than to say she is undead."

Van Helsing gestured, and at his order Seward, and a moment later Quincey Morris, took up screwdrivers and began to undo the coffin's outer sealing.

Arthur, looking on, was swiftly becoming an emotional wreck. " 'Undead'? What does that mean? Jack? Quincey?"

Quincey Morris only shook his head; he was determined at least to get to the bottom of things.

Holmwood continued his protest. "This is insanity! What did poor Lucy do that I should allow this desecration? She died horribly enough—"

Matter-of-factly Van Helsing loosened the last screw and swung the lid of the outer coffin up, revealing the inner casing of airtight lead beneath.

The sight was almost too much for Holmwood.

Striking the screwdriver down through the thin lead sheeting, with a swift stab, Van Helsing created a hole big enough to admit the point of a small fretsaw. Some of his audience drew back— Seward, with his medical experience, was more than half expecting a rush of noxious gases from the decayed body—but nothing of the kind happened, and the professor never stopped for a moment.

He sawed a couple of feet along one side of the lead coffin, then across and down the other side. Taking hold of the loose flange thus created, he bent it back toward the foot of the coffin, stood back a step, and motioned for the others to look.

One by one, with Arthur Holmwood the last to do so, they drew near and peered in. The coffin was empty.

Holmwood, quite pale, backed away from it. "Where is she?" His voice cracked. "What have you done with her, Van Helsing?"

The old man's words fell like the blows of a hammer. "She is vampire. *Nosferatu,* as they say in Eastern Europe. Undead. She lives beyond the grace of God, a wanderer in the outer darkness. They become almost immortal when infected by another *nosferatu.*"

Quincey threw down the tool he had been holding and gave voice to an incoherent groan. It was a sound compounded of outrage and derision, as if he would still refuse to credit what his own experience now compelled him to believe.

But Arthur grabbed Van Helsing. "This is insane! The transfusion of my blood has made Lucy my bride." No one had ever told the intended bridegroom of the other three transfusions, and certainly no one was going to do so now. "I will protect her from this outrage!"

The professor thumped the palm of his hand on the empty inner coffin. The curved lead sheeting sounded hollowly. "As you see, she is not here. The undead must go on, age after age, feeding on the blood of the living."

"Lies! You cannot prove this. Old man! Old lunatic! *What have you done with her?*"

In the next instant Holmwood had actually snatched a revolver from the belt of the surprised Quincey and impulsively leveled the weapon at Van Helsing.

For a long moment shocked silence reigned in the tomb. Quincey Morris was stunned, Holmwood half-mad with grief and bewilderment, the heavy revolver shaking in his hand. Seward, trying to decide how best to restrain Holmwood, was attempting also to retain his grip on his own professional calm. And Van Helsing himself seemed only to await, with stony resignation, whatever fate might send him in the next moment.

Then Van Helsing tilted his head, listening; he raised a hand, imperiously enjoining silence.

In the moments following, the sound of a soft feminine voice singing, crooning a kind of lullaby, came drifting to the men's ears from somewhere not far outside the subterranean vault.

The younger men all stared at each other in wonder.

With commanding gestures Van Helsing continued to enforce silence. Quickly he herded his companions, with their lights, into a kind of recess between old sarcophagi, just out of sight of the stair. As soon as they were all there, he blew out the candles they had been carrying and shuttered the lantern.

In darkness the four men waited, listening, holding their collective breath. Only a faint glow of moonlight came down into the vault through the upper entrance to the crypt. Seward recalled that they had left the iron gate there open.

What he was expecting at that point he could not have said; but not what happened. Presently a white descending figure, cradling something small in both arms and crooning a soft lullaby, became visible in a faint ghostly way upon the stairs.

The figure paused once, giggling in a familiar way, then the lullaby resumed, the white shape once more descending.

Seward could feel his hair rising on his scalp, and Van Helsing's grip tightened like iron on his arm. The voice of the apparition was recognizably that of Lucy—of a woman Seward himself had certified as medically dead, and had seen entombed—but it sounded drunken, almost incoherent, as it sang softly.

At a word from their leader the four men now stepped out from their place of concealment, and Van Helsing drew open the lantern's slide, releasing a beam of concentrated light in the direction of the figure on the stairs.

The face and the red hair of the woman were undoubtedly Lucy's; and in the harsh beam that now fell upon her face all four men could see how her lips were crimsoned with fresh blood, and how the stream had trickled over her chin and stained the purity of the white gown—its fabric now wantonly, carelessly torn at the breast—that was to have been her wedding dress.

With a careless motion, callous as a devil, Lucy flung to the ground the child that up to now she had been clutching strenuously to her breast. Snarling at the men confronting her, exposing inhumanly sharp teeth, she retreated, backing down the remainder of the stairs and maneuvering toward her coffin.

Seward at once darted forward and picked up the child, which cried lustily; dazedly his physician's instincts registered that the babe did not seem to have been much harmed.

The face of Quincey Morris, as he confronted the apparition, was a study in silent horror. By instinct the Texan had drawn his bowie knife and held it ready.

Holmwood had been through too much—far too much—and his knees were buckling.

Now Lucy, actually standing beside her coffin, appeared to take notice, for the first time, of her fiancé's presence in the vault. Immediately, as if by magic, the wantonness and evil faded from her appearance.

She seemed as beautiful and virginal as ever in life, when she advanced on him, saying: "Come to me, Arthur. Leave these others and come to me. My arms are hungry for you. Come and we can rest together. Come to me, my husband, come—"

Seward, dazed with shock, was still capable of registering the fact that there was something diabolically sweet in the tones in which Lucy spoke, something of the tinkling of glass when struck.

Holmwood, moving as in a trance, had started toward her, opening his arms in response to her plea.

"Lucy . . ." he choked.

Van Helsing, as once before, jumped between the couple, this time brandishing a crucifix.

Lucy recoiled, hissing and grimacing, from the object he thrust at her. Never had Seward beheld such baffled malice. He thought that if ever a face meant death—if looks could kill—he saw it at that moment.

Van Helsing, steadily holding up the cross, without taking his eyes from the vampire, demanded of Holmwood: "Answer me now, my friend! Am I to proceed with my work?"

Arthur, groaning, had fallen to his knees, his face buried in his hands. "Do as you will, Van Helsing." His voice was scarcely audible.

As if the crucifix were projecting some invisible, all-powerful force, the old man used it to urge the snarling woman back. Suddenly she leaped, and with a grotesque, unnatural movement in the air, withdrew inside her coffin, vomiting blood upon Van Helsing just before she disappeared.

Several minutes had now passed since Jonathan Harker had left his new wife waiting on the London street.

Mina's fear for her husband's safety, at first acute, had subsided into serious but not desperate worry. She had spent the first minutes of his absence glancing through his journal—the written record of his trip through Transylvania—concentrating particularly upon the later entries, those covering the last days of the period Jonathan had spent as Dracula's guest—or as his prisoner. She still found it impossible to tell which of the horrors related in these entries were to be understood as real, and which were only the products of her husband's disordered fancy.

Mina's efforts to consider the problem calmly were spoiled by a few words her husband had said to her tonight, just before rushing away from the cab. These words kept coming back to her. At each return they seemed more horrifying, more laden with an implication, a suggestion, that so far she was refusing to confront directly.

Jonathan had said: *It is the man himself. The count. I saw him. He has grown young.*

As time passed and Jonathan still did not return, Mina's fears for him mounted steadily. Frequently she looked up from the pages of the horrible journal, on each occasion staring out the window of the hansom cab into the anonymous fog-shrouded throng of London. Every time she looked out for her husband she wondered if she ought to attempt to follow him; but of course if she were to leave the cab, Jonathan might return to it while she was gone. . . .

The instant she heard someone at the hansom's other door, she looked around with quick relief. "Jonathan?"

But when the door was yanked open from outside, it was the prince, her mysterious lover, and not her husband, who confronted her.

When Mina recoiled instinctively, he pleaded: "No—I beg you. I had to see you. I am a madman without you—"

Mina could not speak.

He climbed halfway into the cab, arms reaching for her.

Softly she endeavored to struggle free. "Please—you have no right—my husband—"

"Mina"—and to the woman's ears it seemed for a moment that he had softly added another name—"I have crossed oceans of time to find you. Can you conceive of what I feel for you? It has been a constant search, hopeless, never-ending. Until the miracle happened."

At that very moment, back in the depths of the Westenra family vault, Van Helsing was carefully laying out upon a marble slab his autopsy knives and certain other implements of the specialist. Notable among these last were a wooden stake, more than two feet long and carefully sharpened, the point hardened by charring in a fire, and a heavy hammer, of the type used generally to break up lumps of coal.

The woman in the coffin was unconscious now or comatose, eyes closed. With her pointed teeth, her bloodstained mouth, she seemed to all of the hunters present no more than a nightmare image of Lucy.

Even Arthur's face grew hard as he looked. In a voice containing new strength he asked Van Helsing: "Is this really Lucy's body, or only a demon in her shape?"

The old man grunted. "It is her body—and yet not. But wait awhile, and you shall see her as she was, and is."

When he had arranged all of his implements to his satisfaction, the old man said: "Before we do anything, let me tell you this. When the undead become such, there comes with the change the curse of immortality. They cannot die in the ordinary way, but must go on age after age adding new victims. For all that die from the preying of the undead become themselves undead. And so the circle goes on, ever-widening, like ripples from a stone thrown in the water.

"The career of this so unhappy dear lady as a vampire is but just begun. Those children whose blood she sucks are not as yet so much the worse"—here all eyes turned to the unconscious child in Seward's arms—"but if she lives on, undead, then more and more by her power over them they come to her.

"But if she die in truth, then the tiny wounds of the throats disappear, and they go back to their play, unknowing of what has been."

The professor's voice grew more emotional as he went on. "But most blessed of all, when this now undead be made to rest as true dead, then the soul of the poor lady whom we love shall again be free. She shall take her place with the other angels. So that it will be a blessed hand for her that shall strike the blow that sets her free—the hand that of all she would herself have chosen, had it been to her to choose."

Van Helsing paused, looking at his assembled followers. "Tell me if there be such a one among us?"

All eyes turned to Holmwood.

Holmwood, now having seen for himself the predatory horror—though he was still far from understanding it—had been convinced.

He said to Van Helsing: "From the bottom of a broken heart I thank you. Tell me what I am to do."

The directions were clinical and businesslike. "Take this stake in your left hand, place the point over the heart, and the hammer in the right. When we begin the prayer for the dead, strike, in God's name!"

Holmwood again looked faint. But he accepted—stake in the left hand, hammer in the right—the tools that the professor handed him.

"A moment's courage," the old man assured him, "and it is done!"

Dracula still had his foot upon the step, and his body remained halfway into the cab. Meanwhile Mina had all but given up the hopeless struggle against her own feelings.

Her prince was saying to her: "I lost you once, I'll not lose you again."

She tried to think of Jonathan, but it was hopeless. Mina whispered: "I can't fight my own feelings anymore. . . ."

* * *

Arthur, having positioned the sharp point of the long wooden stake against the whiteness of Lucy's exposed breast, raised the hammer.

And struck hard.

—in London at that instant, Mina to her horror and amazement, saw her lover's eyes go wide. Her prince staggered back from the cab, clutching his chest as if he himself had received a mortal wound. He uttered a hoarse scream: "They deny us!"

—in the crypt, Lucy's eyes flew open with the impact of her true death, and she opened her mouth to scream.

—Mina in London could only watch in fright as a staggering madman retreated from her, losing himself in the crowd, even as he helplessly cried out her name—

—Van Helsing, a strong and determined surgeon, slashing with a huge razor-edged autopsy knife, severed Lucy's head from her body before she could utter a sound.

Dracula had already disappeared into the London crowd.

Mina, more desperate and terrified than ever, was leaning from the window of the cab. "Jonathan!" she shrieked out. "Jonathan!"

Suddenly the door on the other side of the cab was once more jerked open from outside. This time it was Harker, disheveled, bruised, and hatless, who lunged in to take his wife in his arms.

The four men in the crypt, all of them physically exhausted and emotionally drained, were now gathered quietly around the still-open coffin.

Inside it, Lucy now lay in peace. Her head had been restored by the surgeon to its natural place. And Van Helsing with a saw from his bulging tool bag had sawn off the stake close to her breast, the sharp wooden point being left deliberately in the young woman's heart.

The four men together gazed in shame and wonder at her face

of unequaled sweetness and virginal purity. This, their most ideal-
ized memories told them all, was truly how they remembered
Lucy's countenance from the days of her breathing life.

After what seemed an endless silence, Van Helsing, spent and
weary, had five more words to say to Holmwood.

"You may kiss her now."

14

Two days had passed since the heavy coal hammer gripped in Arthur Holmwood's strong right hand had driven the sharp stake through Lucy Westenra's heart, and the surgeon's knife had simultaneously severed the young woman's head from her body.

Today Professor Van Helsing was holding a slightly different knife, though one of approximately the same size. His skilled surgeon's hands were slicing and serving a roast of beef as he entertained two new acquaintances in a private dining room of the grill of the Berkeley Hotel, his residence while in London.

The newlywed Harkers, both Mina and Jonathan, were Van Helsing's guests at this dinner. By now Van Helsing had had the opportunity to read both Harker's journal record of his ill-fated journey to Eastern Europe, and Mina's diary covering the same period of time. In fact both of these volumes now lay on the cloth-covered dining table; the professor had already asked their authors many questions about the contents of these books, and he had several more to ask.

At the moment Van Helsing, between forkfuls of the excellent dinner, was commenting on what he had learned from these records.

"An incredible story, of course, Mr. Harker." A pause to chew and swallow. "But terrible as it is, I have no doubt that your journal is true—I will pledge my life on it. Come, eat! Eat. Another potato? Celebrate your discovery."

Chewing, the professor turned his gaze, twinkling with the joys of food and of discovery, upon his other companion.

"And your dear Madam Mina, who insists I read her diary as well! Ah, she gives me hope there are good women still left to make life happy. Dear Mina, you have a brain that a man should have, were he much gifted, and a woman's heart."

Mina was toying with her food, her heart torn with a raging conflict about which she dared not speak. She did her best to smile at the intended compliment.

Van Helsing chuckled, then paused to lick half-consciously from his fingers a taste of red meat juice from the rare roast; only belatedly did he remember to use his napkin.

His bright eyes probed at Jonathan. "There is a question which I, as a doctor, must ask you."

"Ask it, then."

"In your infidelity with those three demonic women, did you for one instant taste of their blood?"

Harker, startled, dropped his eyes. But without hesitation he shook his head briefly and violently. "No."

Van Helsing relaxed noticeably. "Then your blood is not infected with the disease that destroyed poor Lucy."

The news seemed to relieve Harker of a tremendous weight. In a moment he appeared almost a new man. Reaching for his cane, he started to get to his feet, then sat down again, leaning forward to enter into earnest discussion.

"Doctor, are you sure?"

Van Helsing nodded emphatically. "I would not say so otherwise."

Harker's fist hit the table, rattling the cutlery. "Then thank God! I have doubted everything, even myself—especially myself. I was impotent with fear. You have cured me."

The professor, muttering something soothing, nodded with satisfaction. Then his eyes under their thick sandy brows turned once more to Mina. "And you, my dear madam, are you cured as well?"

She tried to conceal the fact that the question made her acutely uncomfortable. "Cured of what, Doctor?"

Van Helsing's voice was low and calm. He refrained from making any accusations. "Of whatever happened in those pages so carefully cut out of your diary."

Mina stared at the old man defiantly; her husband, still reveling in his relief regarding his own condition, did not appear to have heard the question or grasped its implications.

The young woman remained silent, and for a moment Van Helsing appeared ready to let the matter pass. Then, producing an old gold coin seemingly from nowhere, in the manner of a conjurer, he tossed it on the white tablecloth directly in front of Mina.

When she raised her eyes from the yellow metal to stare at him, the professor calmly informed her: "Your husband has given me this. He found it, and others like it—*there.*"

The coin, lying among grease spots and crumbs on the white linen, had come up heads, and the young woman seemed unable to tear her gaze from the fierce profile of the youthful ruler on its face. In fact she found it horribly, unacceptably, recognizable.

Van Helsing, observing her reactions closely, remarked: "The ancient Prince Dracul himself. He died four hundred years ago— but his body was never found."

Mina was startled from her renewed contemplation of the coin when Van Helsing slapped a piece of meat on her plate, a slice so rare in the center as to be still bloody.

The professor's eyes bored into hers, evidently seeking to discover something. He urged her: "You eat like a bird. Eat. Feast! You will need your strength for the dark days ahead."

Mina looked at her husband. Jonathan had commenced eating heartily now, and seemed stronger than he had been since their reunion in Budapest, much renewed by the good news about his own blood. Meeting his wife's gaze, he smiled and extended his hand, and after an almost imperceptible hesitation she took it.

Still gripping Jonathan's hand, she turned to ask Van Helsing: "Tell me, Doctor, how did Lucy die? I mean—I want to know what happened in the crypt, days after her death certificate was signed.

"I now know the terrible fact—Dr. Seward has told me something—but none of the details. She was my dearest friend, and yet no one has told me. Was she in great pain?"

Van Helsing was deliberately harsh. "*Ja,* I would say so, at first. But after we cut off her head and drive a stake through her heart, she is at peace."

Mina gasped.

It was the first time Harker had heard the horrifying details of Lucy's release. He half rose from his chair, and his voice quavered as he intervened. "That's quite enough, Doctor."

The old man looked at him with sympathy, and his expression softened a trifle. "Enough, perhaps, for the moment. Now you, both of you, must understand why we must find this dark prince

135

and do the same for him. And perhaps you see why there is little time."

Harker slumped back into his chair. His face and voice had hardened. "Fortunately I know where the bastard must be sleeping. In one of the very London properties I helped him to purchase—probably Carfax."

"*Ja,* so I discover from your journal. At Carfax the black devil is Jack Seward's neighbor!"

Pushing dishes, wineglasses, and bottles all aside, reaching impulsively across the table, Van Helsing brought all their hands together, forming a three-way bond.

He said: "We must find your undead count, cut off his head, and stake his heart so that the world may rest from him."

Mina turned pale but said nothing. Van Helsing noted this reaction, though her husband failed to do so.

The handshake concluded, Harker with renewed energy brought out some documents.

He said: "We know that exactly fifty boxes of earth were unloaded from the *Demeter,* and I have already traced some of them to the nine additional properties Count Dracula has acquired in other parts of London. We—or someone—must visit those houses, and make sure the boxes in them are destroyed."

The professor, groping in his pockets for his cigar case, nodded his head. "Dear Quincey, Jack, and Arthur still stand with us. It shall be done."

"But the greater number of those boxes, more than thirty, went to Carfax. I assume they are still there."

Van Helsing nodded again. "And for that reason must we go there. As soon as possible . . . By the way, a story of some interest is in the evening paper."

THE PALL MALL GAZETTE, 3 OCTOBER
THE ESCAPED WOLF
PERILOUS ADVENTURE OF OUR INTERVIEWER
Interview with the Keeper in the Zoological Gardens

. . . After many inquiries and almost as many refusals, I managed to find the keeper of the wolf department. Thomas Bilder lives in one of the cottages in the enclosure behind the elephant house, and was just sitting down to tea when I found him. . . .

When the table was cleared, and he had lit his pipe, he said:

"Now, sir, you can go and ask me what you want. I know what yer a-comin' at, that 'ere escaped wolf."

"Exactly. I want you to give me your view of it. What you consider was the cause, and how the whole affair will end. Now, Mr. Bilder, can you account in any way for the escape of the wolf?"

"All right, guv'nor. I think I can; but I don't know as 'ow you'd be satisfied with the theory."

"Certainly I shall. If a man like you, who knows the animals, can't hazard a good guess, who is even to try?"

"Well then, sir, I accounts for it this way; it seems to me that wolf escaped—simply because he wanted to get out."

From the hearty way both Thomas and his wife laughed at the joke I could see that it had done service before. . . .

I was handing him the agreed-upon half-sovereign when something came bobbing up against the window, and Mr. Bilder's face doubled its natural length with surprise.

"God bless me!" he said. "If there ain't old Bersicker come back by 'isself!"

He went to the door and opened it; a most unnecessary proceeding, it seemed to me. I have always thought that a wild animal never looks so well as when some obstacle of pronounced durability is between us.

After all, however, there is nothing like custom, for neither Bilder nor his wife thought any more of the wolf than I should have of a dog. The whole scene was an unutterable mixture of comedy and pathos. The wicked wolf that for days had paralyzed London and set all the children in town shivering in their shoes, was there in a sort of penitent mood, and was received and petted like a sort of vulpine prodigal son.

Old Bilder examined him all over with most tender solicitude, and said: "There, I knew the poor old chap would get into some kind of trouble; didn't I say it all along? Here's his head all cut and full of broken glass. 'E's been gettin' over some bloomin' wall or other. It's a shyme people are allowed to top their walls with broken glass. This 'ere's what comes of it. Come along, Bersicker."

Shortly after dusk of the same day on which the Harkers had dined with Professor Van Helsing at the Berkeley, a band of five men and one woman had assembled in the secluded grounds of Seward's asylum. Overhead, stark, bare branches showed in lantern light, and dead leaves crackled underfoot; summer seemed to have vanished swiftly from the land.

The spot where the six had gathered was in sight of the window of Renfield's cell, and also within sight of the stone wall, high but readily climbable, which separated the asylum's land from that belonging to the adjoining estate of Carfax. The lightless, decayed bulk of the house at Carfax was not visible by night from where they stood, but its presence loomed in the mind of every member of the band.

Harker, who had put aside his cane for this night's work, stood holding Mina's hand while Van Helsing examined the equipment the others were bringing with them. All the men were dressed for rough work and armed with axes and shovels, as well as knives and revolvers, rifles, torches, and dark lanterns, the latter devices being lamps equipped with tight-fitting shutters that allowed them to be quickly dimmed or brightened. Van Helsing himself had brought a couple of the new portable electric lights, powered by heavy and ungainly-looking batteries.

In addition their leader had provided every member of the raiding party with a necklace of garlic and a crucifix.

Holmwood had also pressed into service for the occasion three scrappy hunting terriers. These dogs whined in anticipation and tugged eagerly at their leashes, and their owner remarked dryly that he feared that in an old building like Carfax rats might be a problem.

Van Helsing, having at least glanced at every item of the party's equipment, finally nodded his approval.

Then, in a hushed voice, he gave the men their final instructions.

"*He* can direct the elements, the storm, the fog, the thunder. He commands the meaner things, the bat, rodent, wolf. He must rest in sacred earth of his homeland to gain his evil powers—and that earth is where we shall destroy him.

"But remember, if we fail here, it is not mere life or death. It is that we become like him, preying on the bodies and souls of those we love best."

Quincey Morris, who had at that moment finished loading his Navy Colt, snapped the heavy weapon shut with a metallic click.

Van Helsing glanced at him. "Mr. Morris, it has been demonstrated that your bullets will not harm him. He must be dismembered. I suggest you use your big knife."

Quincey looked up. "Hellfire, I wasn't plannin' on gettin' that close to him, Doc."

Van Helsing stared. Then, in a nervous reaction to prolonged strain, he began to laugh. His laughter grew, swelled into a roar. Tears came to the old man's eyes.

No one else joined in, and now it was the Texan's turn to stare. He hadn't been trying to make a joke.

Renfield, gripping the bars of his ground-floor window some yards away, was watching and listening with a concentration of maniacal intensity; his keen ears could hear enough of what was being said to catch the general meaning. None of the group took notice of him, or had so much as glanced in his direction.

Jonathan Harker had now drawn his beloved Mina a little apart from the others and was saying good-bye to her—for a little while.

In turn she murmured her love for him, and her determination to be faithful.

Harker might have wondered why the question of fidelity should have arisen now at all—but in fact he scarcely seemed to be listening. Gritting his teeth, he muttered: "I aided that fiend in coming here. And now I must send him back to hell."

On hearing that, Mina looked bleakly unhappy. Days ago her suspicions regarding the identity of her prince had become certainty. "I almost feel pity for anyone—for anything—so hunted as is this count."

Her husband shook his head. "How can you pity such a creature? I brought him here, and now I must send him back to hell. When this task is done, I shall never leave you again."

Then Harker's expression softened as he lovingly kissed his wife, and tenderly gave her into the temporary care of Dr. Seward.

At that, Seward briskly wished his colleagues good hunting, and reminded them he meant to join them as quickly as the press of business would allow. Then he, for once without the pair of sturdy keepers who were his usual escort on the grounds of the asylum, began to conduct Mina back into the building. There, on an upper floor, where Seward himself had his modest living quarters, the housekeeper had already prepared a bedroom and sitting room for her.

After pressing his wife's hand one more time, Harker turned away to join Van Helsing, Quincey Morris, and Arthur Holmwood in their grim, self-chosen task.

* * *

Renfield, observing with great excitement that Mina was about to enter the building, hastened impatiently from his cell's window to its door, where he pressed his face against the bars in an effort to catch another glimpse of her. If only she should happen to come by this corridor—

Renfield's hopes were fulfilled. Within a minute Mina Harker and Seward and the two guards were passing along a hallway within sight of Renfield's cell.

As they did so, the madman called out almost cheerily: "The Master—I smell him! He feeds on the pretty miss."

Mina, startled by an unknown voice that spoke in such clear cultured tones, stopped to stare in confusion at the speaker.

Renfield, much excited by having gained her attention, pressed himself even more frantically against the bars of his door.

He cried: "You're the bride my master covets!"

Seward did his best, short of using force, to hurry Mina along. But she resisted and he had to stop.

"Dr. Seward, who is that man?"

Her escort sighed. "That is, of course, one of my patients—Mr. Renfield. Professor Van Helsing suspects that he is linked somehow to the count."

"Renfield?" Mina was surprised. "The same man who was once Jonathan's colleague?"

"I fear so, yes."

"Then you must let me see him."

Ignoring the doctor's objections, continuing to stare at the yearning madman, she moved back a few steps closer to the cell.

Seward, having given up trying to dissuade Mina from the confrontation, protectively came with her. "Renfield, behave yourself now. This is Mrs. Harker."

Mina was somewhat reassured by her first good look at the man inside the bars. He was, for the moment at least, quite calm and lucid. In fact he gave her a small, almost formal bow as he bade her a good evening.

"Good evening, Mr. Renfield," the young woman responded. She chose to ignore the smell and the appearance of the cell.

And now, as Renfield looked his visitor deep in the eye, his expression began to grow fearful. His voice sank almost to a whisper as he repeated: "You're the bride my master covets!"

Mina's cheeks colored. "You are mistaken. I have a husband. I am Mrs. Harker."

The imprisoned man shook his head, ever so slightly, from side to side, as if he were refusing to believe in any ordinary husband for this woman. He announced: "My master tells me about you."

"What does he tell you?"

Seward, on the verge of intervening, hovered nearby. Renfield for once ignored the doctor. To Mina he whispered: "He is coming . . . he is coming for you."

Then, growing more feverishly excited, he motioned his visitor closer. "But don't stay. Get away from all these men! I pray God I may never see your sweet face again."

Reaching out between the bars so calmly that Mina allowed him to take her hand, Renfield brought it gently to his lips and kissed it. "May God bless you and keep you."

Mina could think of nothing to say, but it was plain that she was deeply disturbed and fascinated.

Then suddenly Renfield erupted, gripping the bars with both hands, smashing his head against them.

He screamed out: "Master! Master! You promised me eternal life, but you give it to the woman!"

At this Mina allowed herself to be hurried away to the upstairs living quarters that had been prepared for her. But the loud cries of the madman followed her. "Doctor Jack! I am no lunatic! I'm a sane man fighting for his soul!"

On entering her suite of sitting room and bedroom, on the first floor above ground level, Mina went immediately to the nearest window, which offered a dim nighttime view of Carfax. Looking out over the stone dividing wall, which was almost invisible amid the bare branches of the intervening trees, she could plainly see the indirect glow of the lights carried by the party of men among whom was her husband.

And now, distantly, she could begin to hear the repeated thud of an ax, swung by strong arms, striking heavy wood.

The men were in deadly earnest, and there was no longer the slightest doubt in Mina's mind as to just whom they were hunting. Her husband's mortal enemy was her own prince and lover. Bloody conflict seemed inevitable; Jonathan might be killed—at *his* hands. Or *he* might die, at Jonathan's—and Mina Harker did not know, could not decide, which outcome would be more terrible.

141

15

The heavy old doors of Carfax had been fitted with new locks, propped up in some cases with new timbers, and barred from the inside against intruders. They were decidedly sturdy doors. But Harker and his three bold companions, wielding ax and steel bars, soon succeeded in forcing an entrance to that ancient house—which still, from the outside, appeared to be abandoned.

Harker and his comrades, on pushing their way into the hall of Carfax through the splintered wreckage of the first demolished barrier, saw by the light of their electric torches and their burning lanterns that the whole place was thick with dust. In the corners were masses of spiderwebs, whereon the dust had gathered till they looked like old tattered rags as the weight had torn them partly down.

The professor paused to contemplate this for a moment. Then he spoke over his shoulder to Harker. Van Helsing's voice was uncharacteristically hushed, like that of a man wary of waking some nearby sleeper.

"You know this place, Jonathan, at least better than we others do. You have photographed it, and copied down the plan."

Harker stood gripping his ax impatiently in both hands. "How bitterly I regret ever having had anything to do with it!"

"*Ja.* Which is the way to the chapel?"

Silently Harker took one of the clumsy electric torches and motioned for the others to follow him.

Despite his earlier study of the floor plan, the layout of the huge house was confusing and the party took a couple of wrong turns. But within a minute, Harker still leading the way, they found their progress halted by a low, arched, oaken door, ribbed with iron bands.

This door, like that at the front entrance, proved to be locked and barred, but again the impatient ax in Jonathan's hands made an effective key.

Behind the oaken door an extensive chamber, vaulted with high Gothic arches, was revealed. Long disuse by any living lungs seemed to have made the air inside stagnant and foul. There was an earthy smell, as of some dry miasma, Harker thought. But no one paid any attention now to such details. Lights flashing about in the hands of the investigators revealed rows of bulky coffin boxes, and a quick tally revealed that there were twenty-nine.

The searchers frowned at one another. There was no need for anyone to state the fact aloud: Unless they should be able to uncover the count here, and destroy him, it would be necessary to seek elsewhere—tomorrow, and for as many days as necessary— for the balance of the fifty.

Harker, his hands resting on the lid of one of the coffins, said in an emotional voice: "I have seen these very boxes at the count's castle. There he was . . . resting in one of them."

The professor grunted. Then, prying energetically, leaning his considerable weight upon a steel bar, he ruthlessly ripped the nailed-down lid from another of the containers. A moment later Van Helsing stood staring at the moldy stuff inside.

After scooping up a handful and throwing it aside, Van Helsing announced: "This is the sacred earth of his homeland. He must rest in it. Destroy every box. Sterilize the earth inside. Leave him no refuge. Let the exorcism begin!"

Harker, once more wielding the big ax, took the lead. He chopped up coffins, splintering their lids, fanatically driving the thick blade into one after another, with cries and gasps of rage. His anger and energy only seemed to increase as the work went on.

Van Helsing had a flask of holy water hanging about his neck, and with it he sprinkled the exposed earth in box after box, chanting: *"In manus tuas, Domine!"*

Into thy hand, O Lord.

Meanwhile Quincey Morris and Arthur Holmwood, having pulled on sturdy gloves, were bending their backs and straining their muscles, opening the boxes as rapidly as Harker splintered them open, dumping out and exposing their moldy contents.

Harker paused for a moment to catch his breath and wipe away the sweat, which, despite the chill atmosphere, was running down his forehead. So far, to his growing disappointment, none of the coffins they had torn open contained the vampire's body. Suppose the fiend should somehow manage to outwit his pursuers?

Never! Taking a fresh stand before another of the boxes, he raised his ax again.

"In manus tuas, Domine . . ." Van Helsing chanted on, alternately sprinkling holy water and crumbling bits of consecrated wafer into the growing piles of Transylvanian soil.

At the asylum, Renfield's painful cries went on and on as if they were never going to cease. Mina, almost directly above him, plugged her ears with her fingers, praying silently that the poor sufferer below might find some kind of peace.

Then she relaxed with a little sob of gratitude; it appeared that this prayer, at least, had been answered.

But she did not know the reason for Renfield's sudden silence. It had been caused by the abrupt appearance of Dracula, in human shape, just outside the window of his cell.

Renfield, on finding himself at last directly confronted by the one he had worshiped so long, for a moment seemed to be entirely struck dumb.

Then, clinging to the window bars, he whispered slavishly to the slender, dark-garbed figure just outside: "Master, Master . . . yes, Master . . . thy will be done."

Renfield paused suddenly, moving his lips in silence. It seemed to him that the figure outside was somehow, wordlessly, conveying its wish to him; and as soon as Renfield understood this, he hastened to grant the wish, to speak the invitation that was necessary before the vampire was empowered to enter this dwelling place.

Quickly he murmured: "Come in, Lord and Master!"

The figure outside inclined its head once, in acknowledgment. It did not appear to move in the ordinary human way; rather it became insubstantial in appearance, and did not turn opaque again until it had drifted in between the bars.

Once inside Renfield's cell, the prince regained solid human form. He stood in the middle of the small space staring coldly at his disciple, and at last spoke to him openly.

"Renfield—you have betrayed me."

The other giggled nervously, insanely. "I tried to warn her, but she would not listen!"

Dracula only stared at him.

Though Renfield now seemed unable to look directly at his long-awaited master, the madman's eyes glowed dangerously. "She must be spared; you cannot have her."

Scornfully Dracula, without deigning to reply, turned his back and would have left the cell through the barred door.

In that moment Renfield, like the lunatic he was, hurled himself upon the vampire.

As soon as he had seen Mina settled into her temporary quarters and had made sure of her security and comfort as well as he was able, Seward went downstairs again. There he heard a report from an assistant and was gratified to learn that there were no problems among the inmates requiring his immediate attention.

Presently Seward equipped himself with heavy gloves and another lantern. After a final word to his chief assistant, he left the building by a rear door and hastened out across the grounds of the asylum, feet scuffing noisily through dead leaves. The young doctor intended to follow his comrades over the wall to Carfax, and there to share whatever dangers they might face, and whatever success they might achieve, in carrying out their work of destruction.

Seward, finding the first ruined door and then following the noise of coffin smashing and the glow of lights, experienced no difficulty in locating his four friends. He had just joined them inside the chapel when they all saw Quincey Morris step suddenly back from a corner of the paved floor he had been examining.

In another moment the men observed, swelling up in that corner, what Harker in his journal later described as "a whole mass of phosphorescence, which twinkled like stars." The bright spots were small eyes, reflecting lantern beams.

All of the men instinctively drew back. The whole place was becoming alive with rats.

The professor, interrupting his labors, cried: "This is *his* doing! Arthur, your dogs! Call them!"

Holmwood immediately blew on a silver whistle he had been wearing on a string around his neck. His trio of terriers, which had been exercising their curiosity by exploring other rooms in the old house, came scampering at once into the abandoned chapel, whining and snarling with their eagerness to fight the rats.

Arthur blew his whistle again, unnecessarily. The terriers were all accustomed to this game, and they all three used the same killing technique, which was swift and efficient: grab the rat, large or small, by neck or back, and lift it off the ground. A quick strong bite, augmented by a savage shake to ensure that the spinal cord was severed, and the lifeless victim was cast aside, to be replaced in a moment by another. For whatever reason, rat-killing dogs were seldom themselves bitten by the enemy.

The floor of the old chapel, already thick with the dust of decades, if not of centuries, was quickly littered with dead rats. Still the scurrying rodents in their ever-increasing numbers seemed to swarm over the place, till the lamplight, shining on their moving dark bodies and glittering, baleful eyes, made the place look like a bank of earth set with fireflies.

The dogs had already shaken the life out of scores of the enemy, but ever-greater numbers of the rats came on. When Seward arrived, the human hunters had been preparing to set fire to a rude woodpile made from Dracula's shattered coffin boxes. Now that plan had to be momentarily postponed while the humans defended themselves against what appeared to be a deliberately planned assault. It seemed to the men that sharp-toothed rodents were springing from every dark corner of the building, coming up out of the earth and out of the night itself, trying to swarm over the men.

The invaders cursed the flea-infested, disease-carrying creatures, plucked them with loathing from their coat sleeves and trouser legs, shot at them with Winchester and pistol, slew them right and left with swords, shovels, and axes.

Van Helsing doused the swarming rodents with holy water; then he tried coal oil, which he had brought along as a means of intensifying fire, and found it at least as effective.

After first making sure of a way out, for themselves and their ferocious allies the terriers, the men set fire to the stacked remnants of the coffin boxes, and gathering the most valuable of their tools and weapons, shielding their faces from the sudden roar of flame, they conducted an orderly withdrawal.

* * *

Back in the asylum Dracula easily overpowered the burly madman. In his rage the prince lifted Renfield bodily from the ground and smashed him several times against the bars of the cell door.

After pausing briefly to observe the result, Dracula went on his way—through that door, moving freely now into the interior of the building.

Renfield, still breathing but fatally injured, lay where he had been thrown down, collapsed against the bars. Pain, numbness, and paralysis, in different parts of his body, made him aware that he had been hideously hurt. Dimly, as through a haze of his own blood, he could see and hear the running feet of several keepers, hastening to his cell to investigate the unusual disturbance.

Renfield muttered: "Her salvation . . . is his destruction. And I am free. . . ."

And with those words he understood that he was dying. It felt like a long dying, going on and on without end.

16

Mina was totally unaware of what was happening in Renfield's cell downstairs, and equally, helplessly, ignorant of what might be going on at Carfax. Once Jonathan and his companions had entered the old house there, even the indirect glow of their lights had ceased to be visible from her window in the asylum.

But whenever she closed her eyes, her active imagination showed her scenes of lurid horror. Even now her prince might be sharing the grisly fate of Lucy—decapitation and the stake. Or her husband might be overwhelmed by the same horror that had already left him gray and trembling, prematurely aged.

If Van Helsing and the others were right, and the prince was really there . . . but Mina had no way of knowing where he was. Dracula had vanished completely from her ken when he disappeared into the crowd along the London street.

If only she could *know* . . . but she could not.

Presently the young woman arose and turned away from her observation post at the window of her small apartment's sitting room. She tottered, exhausted, into the bedroom, and there, without undressing, threw herself down on the bed, telling herself that after a few minutes' rest she would resume her vigil.

Mina Harker was fast asleep minutes before the first red light of the flames at Carfax showed in the nearby window.

Hers was a brief, uneasy slumber, troubled by strange dreams.

And the strangest dream of all was that the prince, Mina's secret, incomparable lover, the man whose destiny seemed to have been entangled with hers for all eternity—the prince himself had somehow come to be with her now, in this very bed in this unfamiliar room on the upper floor of Dr. Jack's asylum.

And in the depth of Mina's dream it seemed to her no more than natural that *he,* the man she truly loved, should be here with her, lying at her side, beginning to embrace her, just as if he and not Jonathan were her true and rightful husband.

In her sleep the young woman murmured helplessly:

"Oh, my love—yes—you have found me."

And *his* voice when he replied was softer than she remembered it, but otherwise just the same.

"Mina . . . my most precious life—"

For the moment, in the glorious freedom of the world of dreams, she could be free of conflict, supremely happy.

Softly she acknowledged: "I have wanted this to happen. I know now that—I want to be with you always—"

Then with a great shock Mina Harker came wide-awake. *This was no dream.* Or rather it was a dream somehow come true. Mina sat up with a gasp.

The presence of the prince, her lover, in the darkness of the bedroom was as firm and real as at any time on any of the occasions since she had met him.

Lying close beside her, he whispered: "Command me, and I will leave you. But no mere mortal man shall come between us. Will you command me to go?"

"No. No, I should, but I cannot. I was so afraid I would never feel your touch again. I feared you were dead—" Mina paused in fearful wonder. "But you are—you can be—no mere man."

In response her beloved prince raised himself to a sitting position and took her hand. Gently he placed her palm under her own breast first.

He said: "Your heart beats, here—" Then he moved her hand to his bare chest: "But here—"

She reacted in silent horror to what she felt; or rather, to what she could not feel. There was no heartbeat.

He told her solemnly: "There is no life in this body."

Mina involuntarily shrank back a little. "But you live. What are you? I must know. You must tell me."

"Can you bear the knowledge?"

"I must. I cannot bear to remain in ignorance."

149

"Very well. I am accounted lifeless, soulless. I am hated, and feared. I have endured oceans of time—committed unspeakable acts—to keep some grip on life, until I could find you."

"No!"

"Yes." His voice pursued her relentlessly. "I am the monster that the breathing men would kill. I am Dracula."

There was a long pause in which Mina remained sitting in the bed, the coverlet pulled around her shoulders as if she were freezing cold. At last she said: "Then the old man is right. It is as I feared. You are the one who held Jonathan a prisoner. And it was you who made dear Lucy—what she became."

Dracula nodded slowly. "I confess those evil deeds, and worse."

"No—"

"Yes! I tell you that without you—without the life, the love you give me—I am dead to all humanity. Without you I am nothing more than a beast that feeds on human blood!"

On hearing this, Mina broke down, flailing her small fists at her lover in ineffective anger. Dracula only averted his face.

But in the next moment she had seized him, clutched at him desperately, with the grip of a drowning woman. "God forgive me! I love you! I do!"

She held her lover gently, stroked his long, dark hair. And the face that Dracula turned again to her was filled with tender and undying love.

At the same time, downstairs in Renfield's cell, a keeper was showing Seward and Van Helsing into the small, barred room where the critically injured patient, his body badly broken, lay on the floor in a small pool of his own blood.

Both physicians were smudged with dust and dirt, their clothing saturated with the smells of age and decay, of rats and smoke. Both were already physically worn from their recently concluded struggle at Carfax. But there was no chance now for either man to rest.

On entering the cell, Seward at once demanded more light, then knelt to pass skilled hands over the fallen figure.

At the doctor's touch, Renfield moaned feebly.

"Back broken, possibly," Seward reported grimly, a moment later. "And certainly cranial fractures. I don't see how he could do this to himself. One injury or the other, perhaps; not both."

Van Helsing, down on one knee nearby, frowned in sympathy with Seward's patient, and joined in the examination.

"Poor devil!" the professor muttered. "We must attempt trephination—to release the intracranial pressure. Quickly! It is our only hope of being able to talk to him."

The lights the doctors had requested soon arrived, in the hands of silent attendants. Seward sent another assistant for surgical instruments.

Moments later Renfield's heavy body had been laid out on the narrow bed where he ordinarily slept. When Seward's bag of medical instruments arrived, he selected from it a sizable two-handed trephine, a tool much resembling a carpenter's brace and bit. With an attendant now holding a lamp, and Dr. Van Helsing supporting Renfield's head, Seward used a small knife to make an incision, loosening a flap of scalp. Then he took up the trephine and began to bore a hole more than an inch in diameter in the back of the unconscious patient's skull.

The trephine made a grating noise as it bit bone. Blood flowed freely from the semidetached flap of Renfield's scalp, soaking Van Helsing's clothing; the professor still gripped the insensible victim, in an effort to prevent some convulsive movement that could be instantly fatal.

Within seconds Seward's efforts were rewarded when a disk of skull came loose, the bone startlingly white in the lamplight. The internal pressure was relieved with another gush of blood.

The patient's body jerked, and for a moment Seward thought that he was dead. But then Renfield's eyes opened, and the physicians leaned close to hear what he might say.

The first words were: "I'll be quiet, Doctor. Tell them to take off the straitwaistcoat. I've had a terrible dream, and it's left me so weak I cannot move. . . . What's wrong with my face? It feels all swollen."

Van Helsing said, in a quiet grave tone: "Tell us your dream, Mr. Renfield."

"Dr. Van Helsing—how good of you to be here. Where are my glasses . . . ? He promised me—eternal life."

"Who did?" Seward demanded.

Renfield seemed not to hear. "But . . . it enraged me to think that he had been taking the life out of her. So when he came to my window tonight, I was ready for him . . . till I saw his eyes." The voice of the dying man was becoming fainter, and his breath more stertorous. "They burned into me, and my strength became like water. . . ."

Renfield's eyes closed again, his life seemed hanging by a thread. Van Helsing urgently commanded an attendant to go for brandy.

Seward, losing control of his own nerves, had put down the trephining drill—it had done its job—and was shaking the helpless body.

"Who do you mean by 'her'? Talk to me, man! Of what woman do you speak?"

Renfield's eyes came open one last time. Obviously his strength was failing fast, and he could utter only a few more words.

"Van Helsing . . . you and your idiotic theories. I warned Doctor Jack. . . . The Master is here, and he feeds on the pretty woman. She is his bride . . . his destruction is her salvation . . . and I . . . *I am free!*"

And with that his body spasmed and died.

At the same time, lying upstairs in the guest bedroom, Mina and Dracula were tenderly, humanly, quietly, making love.

Pulling away restricting garments, eliminating barriers, she whispered softly to him: "No one must ever come between us. I want to be what you are, see what you see, love what you love—"

"Mina—if you are to walk with me, you must die to your breathing life and be reborn to mine."

"Yes, I will. Yes . . ." She gave her assent freely, but without really grasping what the words implied. She was ready to do anything, anything at all, to be with him.

Dracula stroked her hair, the smoothness of her back, her shoulders. He murmured: "You are my love, and my life. Always."

Gently he turned her body, exposing her neck, kissing her throat softly.

Mina moaned and made a tiny grimace of pain as he entered her veins. The pain intensified, at the same time transformed to pleasure, blurred into ecstasy.

Releasing his grip on Mina's throat, an act that brought from her a little moan of loss and disappointment, Dracula sat up straight in the bed. He used his long, sharp thumbnail to open a vein over his own heart.

And faintly now Mina could hear the voice of her true beloved murmuring to her: ". . . and we shall be one flesh . . . flesh of my flesh . . . blood of my blood . . ."

Then, groaning in passion, he pulled her submissive head against his chest. "Drink, and join me in eternal life!"

She drank his blood. She came near swooning as her true lover's life ran into her.

Then, an unexpected shock. The prince faltered at the height of passion and put her away from him.

"What is it?" she demanded thickly.

He said: "I cannot let this be!"

Mina cried out: "Please—I don't care—make me yours—take me away from all this death!"

But suddenly her prince had become bitter and remote. He said: "I lied, to you, to myself. The gift of eternal life is far beyond my power. The truth is, you will be cursed—as I am, to walk in the shadow of eternal death. I love you too much to condemn you!"

"And I love you—" Mina once more pressed her lips against her lover's chest.

At that moment the door of the bedroom burst open with sudden force, framing Van Helsing and the three other hunters, now all returned from Carfax. The professor actually fell into the room with the violence of his entry and had to scramble up from his hands and knees.

Lamps held high in some of the intruders' hands, and light coming from the hallway beyond them, illuminated the couple embracing on the bed. In the doorway the four men froze, Van Helsing still on one knee. They were transfixed by the image of Mina, unclothed, with Dracula's blood around her mouth, her head posed in the very act of drinking from the vampire's veins.

For a long moment there was silence. Then Harker, out of a deep well of desolation and despair, screamed his wife's name.

She recoiled, pulling up the bed covers in an instinctive effort to hide her shame.

At the same instant her illicit lover had undergone a convulsive physical transformation; it was in a grotesque form, midway between that of a human and of a giant bat, that Dracula, snarling with rage, flew to the room's high ceiling, then dove again to confront his persecutors.

In a room now lighted through its window by the mounting

flames of burning Carfax, the men attacked him wildly with their various edged weapons.

Dracula, moving with inhuman speed, wrenched a saber out of the grasp of one of his attackers. Clutching this weapon in a hand that was more than half a claw, the prince parried and fought back, with superhuman strength and skill and quickness, that more than equalized the odds against him.

Twice in those brief but seemingly endless seconds of violence he had the chance to kill one of his opponents—first Seward, then Quincey Morris—but each time Mina screamed and the life of one of Dracula's enemies was spared.

Then Van Helsing, casting aside physical weapons and brandishing a raised crucifix, advanced on Dracula. Boldly the professor confronted his great antagonist, saying: "Your war against God is over. You must pay for your crimes."

His enemy contemptuously threw down his saber. A voice, hissing but intelligible, issued from his deformed throat. "Young fool! You would destroy me with the cross? I served it, centuries before you were born."

The vampire's grotesque forefinger stabbed its pointed nail toward Mina. His bestial eyes, gleaming red, challenged each of the men in turn. "*She,* your best beloved, is now my flesh, my blood, my kin, my bride! I warn you I will fight for her. My armies will fight for her, my creatures to do my bidding—"

"Leave her to God!" the old man commanded. "Your armies are all dead, and we have met your beasts and do not fear them. Now you must pay for your crimes."

Hissing again, Dracula stamped a clawed foot; the cross burst into flame. Van Helsing dropped it, and with his other hand splashed the vampire copiously from his flask of holy water. The liquid striking his monstrous flesh smoked and burned like acid, and Dracula screamed, recoiling. Even as he stepped back he straightened, to take a final, longing look at Mina.

As the men with weapons in their hands rushed at him again, he was transformed before their eyes into a man-sized column of rats, which squealed in a hundred inhuman voices and collapsed into a furry pile, the pile in turn flattening itself at once, dissipating into scurrying black carpet, which in moments had vanished out of the room by every available means of egress.

Silence fell; the enemy was gone, had escaped out of his hunters' reach. The men's weapons, physical and spiritual alike, hung useless in their hands, and they stared at one another with a horror approaching that of ultimate defeat.

Mina still huddled on the bed, trying to cover her shame with bloodied sheets.

"Unclean," she sobbed hopelessly, breaking down utterly at last. "Unclean."

17

By sunrise Mina's hysteria had passed, much to the relief of all the men who still stood ready to die in her defense. All physical traces of last night's horrific incident had been efficiently removed within minutes of the event; clean sheets and quilt had been provided promptly by a staff of servants well accustomed to medical emergencies at any hour. The victim had even slept a little, and by dawn appeared to be recovering—more or less—from at least the short-term effects of her ghastly experience. On that much Drs. Seward and Van Helsing, meeting in almost continuous professional consultation, could agree.

Neither Mina nor any of the men with her had yet really discussed what long-term effects could be expected from her intimate contact with the vampire. The assumption made by all the men was that the intimacy they had observed had been forced by Dracula; and the unhappy woman had said nothing to contradict that idea.

The immediate shock of the experience seemed to have been at least as great for Harker as for his wife; and in the case of her husband the degree of recovery was, in Seward's estimation at least, somewhat more difficult to judge. Harker, in the hours since his discovery of his wife in the vampire's embrace, had for the most part maintained a stoic attitude. Whether he had slept at all was uncertain. He had little to say to anyone, including his wife, and his eyes showed a distant, withdrawn look; his nostrils quivered frequently while his mouth was set as steel.

The young solicitor was suddenly no longer young in his appearance; in a matter of hours Harker's face had become lined and sallow, and Seward was ready to swear that the man's hair had already turned gray at the roots. Without giving any explanation, or offering any comment on his actions to anyone, the outraged spouse had already exchanged his cane for a great curved kukri knife, an East Indian weapon from the big-game hunters' collective arsenal. He now carried this knife with him wherever he went, and had begun compulsively whetting and testing the blade.

So far the Harkers were continuing to occupy the guest suite on the upper floor of the asylum. A sufficient number of spare rooms were available there to accommodate the rest of the party, and for the sake of convenience and solidarity Lord Godalming (to his friends still Arthur Holmwood), Van Helsing, and Quincey Morris had already moved in, or were planning to do so within the day.

All of the men besides Harker had managed to get a few hours of fretful sleep. None could be granted more than that, because of the urgency of the situation.

Van Helsing had undertaken to organize an expedition against Dracula's remaining properties elsewhere in the metropolitan area.

One of these houses was considered by the professor to be of special tactical importance.

"In all probability," the professor counseled his colleagues while standing in Seward's office before a hastily tacked-up wall map, "the key of the situation is in that house in Piccadilly. The count will have deeds of purchase, keys, and other things. He will have paper that he write on, clothing, he will have his book of checks. There are many belongings that he must have somewhere; why not in this place so central, so quiet, where he come and go by the front or the back at all hours, where in the very vastness of the traffic there is none to notice?"

"Then let us go at once!" Harker cried. "We are wasting precious, precious time."

The professor did not move. "And how are we to get into that house in Piccadilly?"

"Any way! We shall break in if need be!"

"And your police; where will they be, and what will they say?"

It was Seward, thinking in a practical mode, who suggested waiting until regular business hours, and then employing a respectable locksmith.

Harker, waving the huge knife he had adopted, urged: "Then

in God's name let us start at once, for we are losing time. The count may come to Piccadilly sooner than we think."

"Not so!" said Van Helsing, holding up his hand.

"But why?"

"Do you forget," he said, with actually a smile, "that last night he banqueted heavily, and will sleep late?"

Mina, who had come into the room to listen to the planners, struggled hard to keep her brave countenance; but the pain overmastered her and she put her hands before her face and shuddered.

It was plain to Seward, looking on, that Van Helsing had not intended to recall her frightful experience. He had simply lost sight of her and her part in the affair in his intellectual effort.

When it struck the professor what he had said, he was horrified at his thoughtlessness and tried to comfort her.

"Oh, Madam Mina! Dear, dear Madam Mina, alas, that I of all who so reverence you, should have said anything so forgetful. These stupid old lips of mine and this stupid old head do not deserve so; but you will forget it, will you not?"

She took his hand and, looking at him through her tears, said hoarsely: "No, I shall not forget, for it is well that I remember. Now, you must all be going soon." Mina, having called upon reserves of strength, was evidently in control of herself, and of the situation—for the time being. "Breakfast is ready, and we must all eat that we may be strong."

Midmorning found Seward, Quincey Morris, Lord Godalming, Harker, and Van Helsing—all five of the men in fact—in London.

On the train going in, Holmwood had said to his companions: "Quincey and I will find a locksmith." Looking at Harker, he added: "You had better not come with us, in case there should be any difficulty; under the circumstances it wouldn't seem so bad for us to break into an empty house. But you are a solicitor and the Incorporated Law Society might tell you you should have known better."

Harker, his figure today wrapped in a cloak to conceal the sheath of the huge knife he wore at his belt, protested that he wanted to share all the dangers and difficulties.

Godalming shook his head. "Besides, it will attract less attention if there are not too many of us. My title will make it all right with the locksmith, and with any policeman that may come along. You had better go with Jack and the professor and wait in the Green Park, somewhere in sight of the house."

"The advice is good!" said Van Helsing. And the matter was so arranged.

At the corner of Arlington Street and Piccadilly, Van Helsing, Harker, and Seward dismounted from their cab and strolled into the Green Park. The day was gray but dry and mild.

Quietly Harker pointed out to his companions the house on which so much of their hope was now centered. The edifice, at 347 Piccadilly, loomed up grim and silent in its deserted condition, among its more lively and spruce-looking neighbors. The three sat down on a bench with a good view of the property and lit up cigars.

The minutes seemed to pass with leaden feet.

At length they saw a four-wheeler drive up to the house. Out of it, in leisurely fashion, stepped Lord Godalming and Morris; and down from the box descended a thickset workingman with his rush-woven basket of tools. Morris paid the cabman, who touched his hat and drove away. Meanwhile Lord Godalming was pointing out to the locksmith what he wanted done.

The workman took off his coat leisurely and hung it on one of the spikes of the railing near the entry, saying something to a policeman who just then sauntered along. The policeman nodded acquiescence, and the man kneeling down placed his bag beside him. After searching through it, he took out a selection of tools.

Then he stood up, looked into the keyhole, blew into it, and turning to his employers, made some remark.

Lord Godalming smiled, and the man lifted a good-sized bunch of keys; selecting one of them, he began to probe the lock, as if feeling his way with it. After fumbling about a bit, he tried a second, and then a third. All at once the door opened under a slight push from him, and he and the two others entered the hall.

The three watchers in the park sat still, Harker puffing furiously on his cigar while Van Helsing's had gone cold altogether. They waited patiently while the workman, holding the door partially open between his knees, fitted a key to the lock. This he finally handed to Lord Godalming, who took out his purse and gave him something. The man touched his hat, took up his tools, put on his coat, and departed; and not a soul, save the three men in the park, had taken the slightest notice of the forcible and illegal entry thus effected.

As soon as the workman was gone, Harker, Seward, and Van Helsing crossed the street and knocked at the door. Quincey Morris immediately let them in. Quincey, too, was now smoking a cigar; because, as he explained, "the place smells so vilely."

Keeping all together, in case of attack, the men moved to explore the house. In the dining room, which lay at the back of the hall, they found eight boxes of earth. With the tools they had brought the men opened these receptacles, one by one, and treated them to deny them as refuge to the count.

On the great dining-room table lay a little heap of keys, of all sorts and sizes—it was an easy assumption that they would be likely to fit the doors of Dracula's other London houses.

Lord Godalming and Quincey Morris, taking from Harker's own records accurate notes of the various addresses in the east and south, took the keys and set out to destroy whatever boxes they could find there.

The other three settled down, with what patience they could, to await their return—or the coming of the count. They paced the uninhabited rooms, or sat gingerly upon the edges of dusty chairs.

The time seemed terribly long while they were waiting. Dr. Seward, observing Harker, was again struck by the change in him. Last night Mina's bridegroom had been a frank, happy-looking man, with strong youthful face, full of energy. Today he was a drawn, haggard old man, whose white hair (in certain lights at least it looked that color) matched the hollow burning eyes and grief-written lines of his face. His energy, however, was still intact; in fact the image that struck Seward was that of a living flame.

Shortly before two o'clock, Holmwood and Morris returned to the Piccadilly house, to report a successful mission, in the East End and elsewhere. All in all, forty-nine of Dracula's fifty coffins had now been denied him.

What to do now?

Quincey gave his opinion: "There's nothing to do but wait here. If, however, he doesn't turn up by five o'clock, we must start off; for it won't do to leave Mrs. Harker alone after sunset."

Van Helsing had just begun to say something about the need for a concerted plan of attack when he stopped speaking and held up a warning hand.

All four men could hear the sound of a key being softly inserted in the lock of the hall door. With a swift glance around the room, Quincey Morris at once laid out their plan of attack, and without speaking a word, with a gesture, placed each man in position. Van Helsing, Harker, and Seward were placed behind the door. Godalming and Quincey stood ready to move in front of the window, should their enemy attempt to escape them by that route.

They waited in a suspense that made the seconds pass with nightmare slowness.

A moment later slow, careful steps could be heard coming along the hall; the count was evidently prepared for some surprise—at least he feared it.

Suddenly with a single bound he leaped into the room, winning a way past his enemies before any of them could raise a hand to stay him. There was something so pantherlike in the movement, something so inhuman, that it sobered them all.

As the count saw them a horrible snarl passed over his face, showing the eyeteeth long and pointed; but the evil smile quickly passed into a cold stare of lionlike disdain.

Harker evidently meant to try whether his lethal weapon would avail him anything, for he had ready his great kukri knife, and made a fierce and sudden cut. The blow was a powerful one; only the diabolical quickness of the count's leap back saved him.

Instinctively Seward moved forward with a protective impulse, holding the crucifix and wafer in his left hand. He felt a mighty power fly along his arm and saw the monster cower back.

The next instant Dracula had swept under Harker's arm before his next blow could fall, dashed across the room, and threw himself at the window. Amid the crash and glitter of falling glass, he tumbled into the flagstoned area below.

Running to the window, the men saw Dracula spring unhurt from the ground, cross the yard, and push open the stable door. There he turned and spoke to them.

"You think to baffle me, you bastards with your pale faces all in a row, like sheep in a butcher's. You shall be sorry yet! My revenge is just begun. I spread it over centuries, and time is on my side. Bah!" With a contemptuous sneer he passed quickly through the door, and his foes heard the rusty bolt creak as he fastened it behind him.

Godalming and Morris had rushed out into the yard, and Harker had lowered himself from the window to follow the count;

but by the time they had forced open the bolted stable door, there was no sign of him.

Realizing the difficulty of following their enemy through the stable, Van Helsing and Seward moved back toward the hall. The first to speak was the professor. "We have learned something—much! Notwithstanding his brave words, he fears us; he fear time, he fear want."

It was now late in the afternoon, and sunset was not far off, with heavy hearts the others agreed with the professor when he said: "Let us go back to Madam Mina—poor, dear Madam Mina. We need not despair; there is but one more earth box, and when we find it, all may yet be well."

Seward could see that he was speaking as bravely as he could to comfort Harker.

On returning to the asylum, the group was welcomed by Mina. On seeing their faces, her own became as pale as death. For a second or two her eyes were closed as if in secret prayer. Then she said cheerfully: "I can never thank you all enough. Oh, my poor darling!" And she took her husband's graying head in her hands and kissed it.

The sky had begun to lighten with the first foreshadowings of dawn when Mina awakened her husband. Her voice and manner were calm and determined. "Jonathan, go, call the professor. I want to see him at once."

"Why?"

"I have an idea. I think that now, only now in this hour before the dawn, I may be able to speak freely—about *him*."

Harker hastened to do as his wife requested.

In two minutes Van Helsing, wrapped in his dressing gown, was in the room, and Morris and Lord Godalming with Dr. Seward were at the door asking questions.

When the professor saw Mina, a positive smile ousted the anxiety from his face. He rubbed his hands together and said: "Oh, friend Jonathan, we have got our dear Madam Mina, as of old, back to us today!" Turning to her, he asked cheerfully: "And what am I to do for you? For at this hour you do not want me for nothing."

At last Mina, in an almost ordinary voice, replied to Van Helsing's question: "It is hard to describe. But *he* . . . speaks to me, without even trying to do so."

The professor nodded. He understood, at least in part.

Quietly, as if the two of them were quite alone, he said to Mina: "Prince Dracula has a strong mind connection to you. He was, in life, a most wonderful man. Soldier, statesman, alchemist—the highest development of science in his time. His heart was strong enough to survive the grave."

Mina searched the professor's eyes, as if to find in them a spark of hope. "Then you admire him."

The old man nodded. "Much so. His mind is great." Then he leaned forward deliberately. "But greater is the absolute necessity to stamp him out. That is why I ask you help me to find him, before it is too late."

Torn with a terrible inner conflict, Mina murmured: "I know that you must fight—that you must destroy him—even as you did Lucy."

Van Helsing, even as he nodded in agreement, sighed in grief and sympathy.

Mina continued in a dead voice: "I know also that I am becoming like him. When I find in myself a sign of harm to anyone I love, I shall die."

The professor's bushy eyebrows rose. "You would not take your own life?"

She nodded, with firm conviction. "I would, if there were no friend who loved me, who would save me such a pain, and so desperate an effort!"

Van Helsing struck the table with his hand. "No, I tell you, that must not be! You must not die by any hand, least of all your own. Until the other, who has fouled your sweet life, is true dead, you must not die, for if he still walks as an undead, your death would make you even as he is. No, you must live!"

Mina's eyes looked in turn at each of the men who were gathered here with her, united by their determination to fight for her. Her gaze seemed to reach them from the great distance of her terrible position as the vampire's victim. First Professor Van Helsing, then her husband—to meet Jonathan's eyes required the greatest effort on her part—then Dr. Seward, Arthur Holmwood, and finally Quincey Morris.

She said to all of them: "And I see that you must fight. *But not in hate*. The poor lost soul who has wrought all this misery is the saddest of all of us. You must pity him, too—as you must me. Why need we seek him further when he is gone away from us?"

"Because, my dear Madam Mina, now more than ever must we find him, even if we have to follow him to the jaws of hell!"

"Why?"

"Because," Van Helsing answered solemnly, "he can live for centuries, and you are but mortal woman. Time is now to be dreaded—since once he put that mark upon your throat!"

Harker sprang forward to his wife's side, as for a moment it seemed that she might faint.

But then with an act of will she rallied. "I want you to hypnotize me!" the woman anxiously declared, speaking to Van Helsing. "Do it before the dawn, for then I feel I can speak, and speak freely. Be quick, for the time is short!"

Without a word Van Helsing motioned for his patient to sit up in bed. Setting his candle on the bedside table, and looking fixedly at her, he commenced to make hypnotic gestures in front of her, from over the top of her head downward, with each hand in turn.

Mina gazed at him fixedly for a few minutes. Seward could feel his own heart beating strongly, for he felt that some crisis was at hand.

Gradually Mina's eyes closed, and she sat stock-still; only by the gentle heaving of her bosom was it possible to see that she was still alive.

The professor made a few more passes and then stopped; his forehead was now covered with great beads of perspiration.

Mina now opened her eyes again, but there was a faraway look in them, and she did not seem the same woman.

By now the men who had been standing in the hallway had come into the room, where they stood crowded around the foot of the bed. Raising his hand to impose silence on them, the professor spoke to Mina in a low, level tone. "His destruction is your salvation, Madam Mina. Help me find him!"

"He is gone," she responded unexpectedly. And added: "I believe that he has now left the country."

"*Ja*," the professor agreed. "Our experienced hunters were busy yesterday. We may be confident we have now destroyed all of his boxes but one." Then quietly he asked: "But how do you know, child, that he is gone?"

"Yes, gone," she whispered presently. "And I must go to him. I have no choice. He calls."

The old man glanced at the onlookers, silently urging them to remain quiet. Then he waited a little longer, until he was satisfied that the trance was deep enough.

At last he asked Mina softly: "Where are you going?"

Long moments passed before she whispered in reply: "Sleep has no place to call its own—I am drifting, floating."

"Where?"

"Going home . . . home."

The professor took thought, frowning and pulling at his lower lip. "What do you hear?" he tried.

Another pause. "Mother ocean," the young woman replied at last. "I hear lapping waves, as on a wooden hull . . . rushing water. Creaking masts . . ."

The professor turned in hushed elation to his male colleagues. Fiercely he whispered: "Then truly we have driven him from England!"

Hushed exclamations broke from the other men. Spontaneously they edged a little closer to Van Helsing and his patient.

After a glance at Mina, which told him that she was emerging spontaneously from her trance, the professor clenched a fist and spoke in a more normal voice.

"God be thanked that we have once again a clue! The count saw that with but one earth box left, and a pack of men following like dogs after a fox, this London was no place for him. This means he have take his last earth box to board a ship, and he leave the land. Tally-ho, as friend Arthur would say.

"Our old fox is wily; but I, too, am wily, and I think his mind in a little while."

By this time Mina's eyes were fully open again and she was listening, nodding slowly in agreement.

Seward, looking on from a little distance, noted grimly that already, with hideous swiftness, this latest victim of the vampire was turning gaunt and pale, her gums receding from her teeth. In his opinion the process of transformation was even now well advanced.

18

The Harkers were badly in need of rest, as were the small determined band of men who would protect the couple and avenge their injuries. But before any of the group could rest in anything like peace, it was necessary to do all that could be done to verify the report Mina had given under hypnosis. Therefore as soon as full daylight came, the four men other than Jonathan paid a visit to the London docks.

That evening, back in the asylum, Van Helsing reported to the Harkers on the results of this expedition.

"As I knew that he, Prince Dracula, wanted to get back to Transylvania, I felt sure that he must go by the Danube mouth; or by somewhere in the Black Sea, since by that way he come.

"And so with heavy hearts we start to find what ships leave for the Black Sea last night. He was in sailing ship, since Madam Mina tell of masts and sails . . . and so we go, by suggestion of my Lord Godalming, to your Lloyd's insurers, where are note of all ships that sail.

"There we find that only one Black Sea–bound ship go out with the tide. She is the *Czarina Catherine,* and she sail from Doolittle's Wharf for Varna, and thence on to other parts and up the Danube. And there are those who remember seeing the heavy box, of coffin shape, being loaded on board her, and the tall man, thin and pale, with eyes that seem to be burning, who see that the box is loaded.

"And so, my dear Madam Mina, my dear Jonathan, it is that we can rest for a time, for our enemy is on the sea."

The Harkers exchanged a look and nodded; this news was no surprise.

Van Helsing continued: "To sail a ship takes time, go she never so quick; and we go on land more quick, and we meet him there. Our best hope is to come on him in the box between sunrise and sunset; for then he can make but little struggle, and we may deal with him as we should."

For the first time in many days, the Harkers and their friends were now able to sleep with something like a sense of security; and the first day after their confirmation of Dracula's departure was spent in resting and regaining strength.

Then the preparations for the next phase of the battle went forward apace.

But all was far from satisfactory. On the fifth of October Van Helsing said to Seward: "Friend John, there is something you and I must talk of alone, just at the first at any rate. Later, we may have to take the others into our confidence."

"What is it, Professor?" Though Seward was afraid he knew.

"Madam Mina, our poor, dear Madam Mina is changing."

A cold shiver ran through Seward to find his own worst fears thus endorsed.

Van Helsing continued: "With the sad experience of Miss Lucy before us, we must this time be warned before things go too far. I can see the characteristics of the vampire coming into her face. It is now but very, very slight. Her teeth are some sharper, and at times her eyes are more hard."

Seward thought that "very slight" might be too optimistic a view, but at the moment he was not disposed to argue.

The professor went on: "Now my fear is this. If she can, by our hypnotic trance, tell us what the count see and hear, is it not more true that he, who have hypnotize her first, and who have drink of her very blood and make her drink of his, should compel her mind to disclose to him what she know?"

Seward reluctantly nodded acquiescence. "Yes, including our plans for hunting him."

"Then what we must do is keep her ignorant of our intent, and so she cannot tell what she know not. This is a painful task; but still it must be. When today we meet, I must tell her that for reason we will not speak she must not more be of our council, but be simply guarded by us." The professor wiped his forehead, which had broken out in perspiration at the thought of the pain he might have to inflict upon the poor soul already so tortured.

But when it came time for the day's strategy session in Dr. Seward's study, Mrs. Harker sent a message by her husband to the rest of Dracula's foes.

Jonathan, on entering the room where they were waiting for him, reported: "Mina tells me that she believes it better that she should not join us at present. She says in that way we shall be free to discuss our movements without her presence to embarrass us."

Van Helsing and Seward exchanged a look; both physicians were relieved.

With that question apparently settled, the men began at once planning the campaign. Van Helsing put the facts before his associates.

"The *Czarina Catherine* left the Thames yesterday morning. It will take her at the quickest speed she has ever made at least three weeks to reach Varna, on the Black Sea; there is the Atlantic and the whole Mediterranean she must traverse. But we can travel overland to the same place in as little as three days.

"Now, if we allow for two days less for the ship's voyage, owing to such weather influences as we know the count can bring to bear, and if we allow a whole day and night for any delays which we may suffer, then we have a margin of nearly two weeks. Thus, in order to quite safe, we must leave here on seventeenth October at latest. Then we shall be sure to be in Varna on the day before the ship arrives; of course, we shall all go armed—against evil things, spiritual as well as physical."

On the morning of the sixth of October, Mina woke her husband early and asked him to bring Dr. Van Helsing. Harker thought it was another occasion for hypnotism, and at once went for the professor.

On reaching Van Helsing's room, he found the professor already dressed and the door of his room ajar, as if he had expected some such call. The old man came to the Harkers' rooms at once, and asked Mina if the others might come, too.

"No," she said quite simply. "It will not be necessary. You can tell them just as well. I must go with you on your journey."

Dr. Van Helsing was as startled as the lady's husband. After a moment's pause the professor asked: "But why?"

"You must take me with you. I am safer with you, and you shall be safer, too."

"But why, dear Madam Mina?"

"I can tell you now, whilst the sun is coming up; I may not be able again. I know that when the count wills me, I must go to him. If you leave me here in England, and he tells me to come to him in secret, then I must—using any device to hoodwink—even Jonathan."

With that last word, she turned upon her husband a look filled with bravery and love. Harker's eyes filled with tears, and he could only clasp her hand.

"Madam Mina, you are, as always, most wise. You shall with us come; and together we shall do that which we go forth to achieve."

The penetrating gaze of the professor lingered, and Mina returned it calmly. What she had just told him had been no worse than a half-truth; the full truth would have included the fact that she yearned desperately for reunion with her vampire lover. There were hours when she found herself shamelessly ready to abandon her husband, even her life, to be with Dracula.

It was on the morning of the twelfth of October that Dracula's six pursuers at last left London, riding the boat-train that brought them to Paris on the same night, where they took the places they had reserved aboard the Orient Express.

Three days after leaving Paris, they were all aboard a private railcar jolting slowly eastward across Bulgaria toward the port of Varna on the Black Sea. Mina was now lethargic, sometimes even comatose, through most of the daylight hours. At dawn and dusk, when she could most easily be hypnotized by Van Helsing, her murmured comments still indicated that the count was progressing steadily toward his home by ship.

Today, on awaking around midmorning, she found that the train had stopped. That, she thought, was according to plan; they would be on a siding now, near Varna, waiting for the latest word concerning the movements of their quarry.

For the moment Mina and Jonathan were alone in the small

private compartment they shared. He was staring out the window, and the only sound was the endless whisper of the whetstone with which he repeatedly stroked the curved steel of the murderous weapon he had adopted.

For a time she lay regarding her husband silently. This was a far different man from the young solicitor to whom she had once become engaged—that seemed a lifetime distant. She thought now that every day his hair, at roots and temples, was grayer than it had been the day before. The process must have begun from the moment when he had discovered her in her lover's arms.

Suddenly, overwhelmed by her own feelings, Mina burst out: "My poor dear Jonathan, what have I done to you?"

Startled, Harker turned from the window. Putting down knife and whetstone, he was all tenderness and concern as he attempted to console his wife.

"No . . . no . . . no . . . *I* have done this to both of us." And even as the young man spoke, his imagination continued to torment him with visions of the three fiendish, lascivious women, tempting and shaming him at the same time.

Fiercely he commanded himself to think of other matters, of anything instead of *that.*

He asked: "Where is he now?"

Mina closed her eyes. Her voice sounded both helpless and hopeless. "He is at sea—somewhere. I can still, whenever I am hypnotized by the professor, hear the waves lapping against his ship. The wind is high." She paused, then added bleakly: "He calls me to him."

Her husband swallowed, considering this. Then he made his wife a solemn pledge: "Mina. If you die, I will not let you go into the unknown alone."

In another section of the same private car, a large central compartment that had been furnished as a kind of parlor or sitting room, Seward sat staring listlessly out a window into the gray gloom of the autumnal Bulgarian countryside, here on the edge of the city of Varna. Meanwhile Quincey Morris, in his cold-weather western garb, including a sheepskin jacket, busied himself with preparations for the last phase of the hunt.

At the moment he was using his bowie knife to sharpen several wooden stakes, each as thick as his wrist. This compartment, like most of the others in the car, was heated by a wood stove standing in one corner, vented by a metal chimney to the outside, and secured with taut wires to keep it from tipping. And in this stove Quincey had built up fire enough to char the sharp points of his stakes to the desired hardness.

Also near at hand, stacked in another corner of the compartment, stood four Winchester rifles, which the Texan had recently been cleaning and oiling, along with their supply of ammunition.

In the middle of the room space, a large table under a ceiling lamp held a spread-out map, along with train schedules, notes, copies of various cabled messages, and a pocket watch inexorably ticking away the hours.

A door opened and Lord Godalming came in, waving a copy of the latest cable that had just been brought to the train by special messenger from the British consulate in nearby Varna. Holmwood remarked: "We have reached Varna ahead of the *Czarina Catherine* and her devil's cargo."

At that Seward, who had been sitting tensely idle, snatched up and examined the contents of the telegram. He noted that the message was directed: "from Rufus Smith, Lloyd's, London, to Lord Godalming, care of H.B.M. Vice-Consul, Varna."

Harker, his kukri knife in hand as usual, now entered the compartment. When the others looked up to hear what news he might bring, he gloomily and tersely reported that "Mina is worse every day."

The men, exchanging glances among themselves, murmured such expressions of sympathy as they could find.

Harker did not seem to hear them. "Even so," he said, staring out the window, "I no longer fear this monster. I will kill him myself with the first blow."

He sat down next to Quincey, near the window, and took out a whetstone to resume sharpening his knife.

No more than a few minutes passed before a messenger on horseback pulled up beside the stopped train. Soon Holmwood was opening another wire, this one quite disturbing, from his clerk at Lloyd's.

This one Godalming read aloud, in a bitter voice, to his colleagues in the hunt. The news was that Dracula had, at least for the time being, outwitted and bypassed his pursuers, by causing the ship that bore him to sail past Varna in the night, to the port of Galatz, also on the Black Sea, but farther to the north and east.

171

Quickly the council of hunters—with the exception of Mina, who had not yet joined them today—regathered around the table spread with maps and schedules.

With stabbing motions of his forefinger, Harker indicated first Dracula's presumed position now, near Galatz, and then their own, at or just outside the city of Varna. The two were at least two hundred English miles apart by mail.

Holmwood had ordered the latest messenger to stand by; now the English lord hastily began to write out the communications necessary to get their private car moving again, toward Galatz, as rapidly as possible. The journey would take them through Bucharest.

Meanwhile Harker, more haggard than before—Seward noted that his hair was now certainly beginning to turn white—said to the others with fierce energy: "Once we get to Galatz, we'll follow the bastard upriver on horseback—cut him off. He must not be allowed to reach the castle!"

While a locomotive was found and connected to their car, and the next leg of their journey commenced, the group drew up their plans in considerable detail. When it should become necessary to leave the railway, Dr. Seward and Quincey were to carry on the pursuit on horseback while Jonathan and Lord Godalming hired a steam launch and took it up one of the rivers; Holmwood was experienced in such boating. Of course much might depend on their choosing the correct route.

The various contingencies under which the four men might later recombine their forces were considered.

Again, their final decision in this matter would depend upon what route Dracula, or those who carried him, might choose to take.

While these plans were being made, Mina joined the company, receiving, as usual, a courteous if subdued welcome.

And Van Helsing assured the other men: "Be not afraid for Madam Mina; she will be my care, if I may. I am old. My legs are not so quick to run as once; and I am not used to ride so long or to pursue as need be, or to fight with lethal weapons. But I can fight in other way, and I can die, if need be, as well as younger men.

"I will take Madam Mina right into the heart of the enemy's

country while the old fox is tied in his box, floating on the running stream whence he cannot escape to land—where he dares not raise the lid of his coffin box lest his carriers should in fear leave him to perish. We shall go in the way where Jonathan went, from Bistritz over the Borgo, and find our way to the castle of Dracula. There is much to be done so that nest of vipers be obliterated."

Harker, showing emotion more openly than he had in days, was aghast, "Professor, do you mean to say that you would bring Mina, in her sad case and tainted as she is with the devil's illness, right into the jaws of his death trap?"

Van Helsing raised his chin as if accepting a challenge. "Oh, my friend, it is because I would save Madam Mina from that awful place that I would go. Remember, as she herself has warned us, if she is left unguarded, he may summon her to him.

"And if the count escape us this time—and he is strong and subtle and cunning—he may choose to sleep him for a century. And then in time our dear one"—here Van Helsing took the hand of Mina, who was staring at him hopelessly—"would come to keep him company, and would be as those others that you, Jonathan, saw.

"Forgive me that I make you so much pain, but it is necessary. My friend, is it not a dire need for which I am giving, if need be, my life? Be not afraid for Madam Mina. It is she who will protect me."

For a moment Jonathan, now in hopeless confusion, only stared at the old man. Then the suffering husband gave a fatalistic shrug. "Do as you will. We are in the hands of God. And may God give *him* into *my* hands, just long enough to send his soul to burning hell!"

19

Relentlessly the pursuit continued.

Lord Godalming, by exercising to the utmost all the influence he possessed, both at the consulate and by telegram, had been able in the amazingly short time of a few hours to have the private car attached to another train. The party of adventurers got started for Galatz sooner than any of them had really dared to hope. Anxiously they pored over their maps, plotting the route by rail from Varna to that city. It seemed straightforward enough, though indirect, requiring a large jog through Bucharest—but to their consternation unforeseeable railroad difficulties in the vicinity of that latter city, in the early hours of the morning, caused them some delay, about which wealth and influence could do nothing.

Galatz, when they finally reached it on the morning of the following day, proved a more modern town than any of the travelers had expected. Electric lights illuminated portions of the waterfront, and many of the streets were paved. Immediately upon arrival, while the Harkers undertook to remove the baggage from the private car and establish rooms for the party in a hotel, the other men moved aggressively. It seemed futile to hope that Dracula would still be here within their reach, yet they dared not discount the possibility.

Lord Godalming and Professor Van Helsing soon prevailed upon Messrs. Mackenzie and Steinkoff, agents of the London firm of Hapgood, to allow them to go on board the *Czarina Catherine*, which lay at anchor out in the river harbor.

Captain Donelson of the *Czarina*, a Scot, had no objection to entertaining visitors. He told them, as if he were eager to recount the miracle to someone, of the amazingly favorable conditions his ship had enjoyed throughout the voyage from London.

Yes, the captain remembered very well the shipment in which his callers were interested: one large, coffinlike box. This item of cargo had indeed been aboard, but it had been unloaded hours ago, consigned to one Immanuel Hildesheim in Galatz.

Hildesheim, when located in his office, said he had received a letter from a Mr. de Ville of London, asking him to receive the box and give it in charge to a certain Petrof Skinsky, who dealt with the Slovaks who traded inland, by means of riverboats, to this port on the Black Sea.

Hildesheim had been paid for his work on behalf of his London client by an English bank note, which had been duly cashed for gold at the Danube International Bank.

The hunters sought for Skinsky, but were unable to find him. One of his neighbors said that he had gone away two days before, and this was corroborated by Skinsky's landlord.

Even as the men were talking in Hildesheim's office, another of the local people came running in and said that the body of Skinsky had been found in a nearby churchyard, and that his throat had been torn open as if by some wild animal.

The Englishmen and their Texan friend hurried away lest they should be in some way drawn into the affair, and so detained.

With heavy hearts they rejoined the Harkers at their new hotel in Galatz.

All the evidence, including Mina's continued communications in hypnotic trance, and also the information gathered in Galatz, pointed to the same conclusion: that their quarry was even now continuing his journey by riverboat; but by exactly what route Dracula was traveling was still uncertain.

While the men took half an hour's needed rest, Mina, examining the courses of the local rivers shown on the map, decided that either the Pruth or the Sereth would provide a possible route.

She was soon ready to deliver a report in both written and oral form. "The Sereth is, at Fundu, joined by the Bistritza, which runs up around the Borgo Pass. The loop it makes is manifestly as close to Dracula's castle as can be got by water."

At the next strategy meeting, their plans for the last phase of the pursuit were soon set in final form and put in motion.

* * *

A day or so later, Harker wrote one entry in his continuing journal after dark, by the light from the furnace door of the rented steam launch. He and Holmwood, according to plan, were headed up the Sereth, looking for the mouth of the Bistritza, as Mina had suggested.

Harker wrote: "We have no fear in running at good speed up the river at night; there is plenty of water to avoid running aground, and the banks are wide enough apart to make steaming, even in the dark, easy enough.

"Lord Godalming"—Harker, not long ago a mere solicitor's clerk, still felt uncomfortable speaking of his social betters with informality—"tells me to sleep for a while, as it is enough for one to be on watch. But I cannot sleep—how can I with the terrible danger hanging over my darling, and her going out into that awful place. . . . My only comfort is that we are in the hands of God."

His journal continued:

31 October. Still hurrying along. The day has come, and Godalming is sleeping. The morning is bitterly cold. As yet we have passed only a few open boats, but none of them had on board any box or package anything like the size of the one we seek. The boatmen were scared every time we turned our electric lamp on them, and fell on their knees and prayed.

1 November. No news all day. We have found nothing of the kind we seek. We have now passed into the Bistritza, and if we are wrong about our quarry's plans, our chance of overtaking him, on water at any rate, is gone.

We have overhauled every boat, big and little. Early this morning, one crew took us for a government boat and treated us accordingly. We saw in this a way of smoothing matters, so at Fundu, where the Bistritza runs into the Sereth, we got a Romanian flag—three vertical strips, of blue, yellow, and red—which we now fly conspicuously, and since then have held every deference shown us, and not once any objection to what we ask or do. Some of the Slovaks tell us that a big boat passed them, rowing at more than usual speed as she had a double crew on board. . . .

Even though the river flows directly below the castle (I shall never forget a detail of the geography of this damned place), it must be far too rough at that point, and for some miles downstream, for any boats. The count will have to travel overland on the last miles of his journey; so I cling to the hope that we can make our planned rendezvous with Mr. Morris and Dr. Seward, and that they will have with them the necessary extra horses.

The first days of November were bringing snow and bitter cold to the high Carpathians.

On the seventh of that month, a wagon loaded with a single box the size of a large coffin, driven and guarded by mounted Gypsies, was racing over a mountain road toward Dracula's castle, now only a few miles away. Inside the box a single manlike form, garbed now in a rich robe as if for some important ceremony, rested upon a packing of earth. Dracula was almost comatose with daylight, inactivity, and the lack of recent feeding. His long hair was now white, his age-wrinkled face and hands almost the same color.

At the same hour, on a nearby road high in the Borgo Pass, Van Helsing was driving another wagon, with Mina as his passenger. Two horses had been enough for these travelers when they left Galatz; but later, after one of their several changes of horses at inns and rest stops, they made better time with, as Mina described the arrangement, "a rude four-in-hand."

The professor was wrapped in furs against the wintry day, and he was very tired, struggling to stay awake as he held the reins.

Mina was on the seat beside the professor, her body slumped against his, as she continued her new habit of spending most of the daylight hours in slumber. She also was wearing furs, and in addition her protector had covered her with a thick lap robe or rug.

But suddenly without any apparent cause, the young woman was wide-awake. Her manner was animated, filled with an almost childlike excitement.

The professor made no comment about this abrupt awakening, but in a moment he thought he could see what he thought must be its cause: a towering stone structure that could only be Dracula's castle had just come into view, on a high crag ahead.

Mina, looking around her now in every direction, murmured in an excited voice: "I know this place."

The ancient crucifix of a roadside shrine looked down upon the turning in the road. The figure on the cross was much worn and splintered away by time and weather, the blasphemous ambiguity of its wolf's-head image now difficult to see.

And indeed even Van Helsing failed to notice the peculiarity of this image.

"The end of the world," he remarked. Certainly the scene,

particularly the even higher country ahead of the travelers, looked gloomy, frozen, desolate.

"We must go on!" his passenger urged him. She was continuing in her state of quiet excitement.

The professor, troubled by this exuberant reaction, studied his young charge.

After a moment he shook his head. "It is late, child. Better I build a fire, and we rest here."

"No, I must go! Please, let me go!" Such was Mina's vehemence that it seemed only a physical struggle could hold her back.

Rather than attempting anything of the kind, the old man reluctantly drove on.

At last he pulled the horses to a stop in a small clearing on level ground no more than a couple of hundred yards below the castle. Having come this close, Mina was content to rest and wait; and here her guardian, moving quickly as night was coming on, established a kind of camp. With plenty of dead wood available here, he built up a roaring fire. And around this campfire Van Helsing, using crumbled holy wafers and holy water, traced a wide circle on the hard earth with its thin covering of snow.

Then, moving wearily, but still glad of the chance to keep moving in the cold, Van Helsing prepared some food; fortunately they had been able to obtain fresh supplies at several places on their journey.

Mina, meanwhile, seemed to become ever more awake and alert, obviously energized by the night. She sat on her haunches, in a pose he found disturbingly, ominously unladylike, watching Van Helsing with a look of bright anticipation. All traces of her long suffering, and of weariness, seemed to have dropped away.

When the contents of the pot resting by the fire were hot—it was leftover stew, carried frozen from the day before—Van Helsing ladled some into a bowl and brought it to Mina.

"You must eat something, child."

"Why have you now begun to call me 'child'?"

He did not answer.

She accepted the bowl from Van Helsing's hands, but then, to his silent concern, only set it down beside the fire.

"I am not hungry." The young woman's voice sounded wide-awake but quite remote.

The old man was displeased at this reaction, but he was not at all surprised. Without comment he returned to his own place on the other side of the fire—still carefully within the circle. There he sat on a piece of wood, a little warmer than sitting in the snow, eating from his own bowl and watching his young charge uneasily.

At that moment, from somewhere not very far outside the circle of firelight, there came a sound that gave him the sensation of his hair standing up; as if someone had drawn an icy finger down his spine. What he heard was the soft, silken, tingling sound of feminine laughter, almost unbearable in its exquisite sweetness. . . .

The old man was afraid to look around. It chilled him to see the expression on Mina's face. It was a bright look, not at all fearful. Her eyes were interested—yes, even amused—as she gazed over Van Helsing's shoulder, at something—or someone—she was evidently able to see quite plainly in the snowy darkness.

Just back there over his shoulder—somewhere quite nearby in the snow, and in the night—three feminine voices ceased to laugh. Now they spoke, in a language Van Helsing could understand, though he had not heard it spoken for many years:

"You, sister by the fire—you take him first—but leave some sweets for us—"

"He is old, but stout. There will be kisses for us, too—"

"We will all feast, before the Master comes—"

The professor felt quite certain that Mina in her present state, though ordinarily she did not know the ancient tongue, was quite capable of understanding what was being said to her by these women, these vampires who claimed to be her sisters. Still she did not appear to be paying them any particular attention. It was almost as if she could not hear them at all, or—ominously—was pretending she could not.

Mina's gaze, eerily cheerful but sympathetic, had come to remain fixed upon Van Helsing.

He tried to speak, but his mouth was dry, and for once he could not think of anything to say.

Now suddenly his companion bounced—there was no other word for such an animal movement—shifting her weight on the log where she was sitting. And with the movement, her fur robe opened as if by accident, and the upper part of her inner clothing parted as well. Suddenly one of her breasts had become completely revealed, but Mina seemed completely unaware that this had happened—or else she was utterly indifferent to the fact.

Her red lips parted in a smile, strongly suggested that she was not so indifferent after all. In the next moment she arose suddenly, a sinuous and graceful movement, and came around the fire to Van Helsing's side.

He did not move, he thought he dared not speak. He seemed unable to tear his eyes from the young woman's partially exposed body. With some remote portion of his mind the old professor was aware that this was very like what Jonathan Harker had experienced in the castle; this was what the vampire's victims always felt.

Mina sat down very close to him. Her attitude was not so much flirtatious as friendly, conversational.

"You are so good to me, Professor. I want to do something for you in return . . . something that will give you joy." After allowing him to consider that for a moment, she added: "Shall I tell you a secret?"

"What?" It required a tremendous effort to get out even a single word.

"It's about Lucy." Mina's dark eyes twinkled with silent laughter. "She harbored secret desires for you. She told me so. And you must have secret thoughts, wishes, of your own. . . . I, too, know what men desire."

At first Mina's touch upon Van Helsing's shoulder, his arm, his hair, was almost motherly. Gently she pulled his head down into a position where he might rest against her. How badly he needed rest! But then at once—why had he not understood, a moment ago, that this must happen?—her bare breast, the nipple erect, was pressed against his cheek, between his lips. . . .

Perhaps it was only the mocking background laughter of the three demonic women that enabled him to break the spell. With a hoarse cry, exerting all his strength, Van Helsing managed to struggle free of Mina's embrace. With shaking hands he fumbled into an inner pocket of his coat, extracted a tin box, and from it produced a holy wafer.

Now he was free to speak, to pour out words into the night. "*Domine, Christos*—Lord Christ, bless this child! Deliver her from evil—"

Van Helsing's pressing of the wafer to Mina's forehead, a gesture meant as benediction, had instead an effect that caused him to instinctively recoil. Her soft skin seared at the touch, as if the Sacrament had been a red-hot iron.

Mina, her forehead now branded by a scarlet mark, reeled back screaming.

"I am *his!*" she cried out. And a moment later she lay on the cold ground, gasping.

Van Helsing, moving on instinct, hastened to reinforce his sacred ring with holy water that had almost frozen in its flask.

When the flask was empty, he, too, collapsed, muttering to Mina: "I have lost Lucy. I will not lose you."

Dracula's women, prowling baffled outside the circle, hissed at him: "None is safer from us than her. She is our sister now!"

Raising his head and shoulders, the professor summoned up enough energy to curse them. "Bitches of the devil! Satan's whores! Leave us, this is holy ground!"

Enraged and frustrated by his defensive measures, the three vampire women rushed at the horses. The horses whinnied and cowered, and moaned in terror and pain as humans do—but they could not escape. Van Helsing had to watch them being torn to bloody bits while all the time the women laughed. They took a long time with their sport, killing the four horses as painfully as possible, and he looked on helplessly until his senses failed him.

20

The professor awoke a little after sunrise, shivering with cold even inside his several layers of fur. For a long moment he did not know where he was, or what he had been doing; then the nightmarish reality of his position returned to him.

Mina, he saw to his vast relief, was sleeping quietly, decently and warmly wrapped in her furs, and still within the circle of protection. Slowly, stiffly, the old man got himself erect, brushing snow from his furs. Very carefully Van Helsing approached Madam Mina, bent over her as she slept, and reached out a hand to put back the fur hood, and her own dark hair, from her forehead.

Yes, it was as he had feared.

In the place where the Host had touched her skin, the devil's mark now burned, scarlet as sin itself.

The professor thought that she, contaminated with the vampire's blood, would not be able to pass out of the holy circle unaided now, any more than those three women had been able to pass in.

Those three were out of his sight and hearing now. They had retreated, as he had expected they would have to do, with the coming of the sun. And Van Helsing knew, from Harker's account of his experiences in the castle, exactly *where* they must have gone. And he knew what he himself must do now—the terrible things he had come here to do.

Well, last night's perils, culminating in the sadistic slaughter of the horses, had nerved him for the effort—if indeed his determination had needed any reinforcement.

Moving on cramped limbs, slow and numb with cold, he built up the fire, which was almost dead. For once the thought of food disgusted him, but he knew that he would need his strength.

Averting his eyes from the mangled bodies of the horses, Van Helsing went to the wagon and from the wrapped-up stores it contained got bread, and dried meat, and a flask of brandy.

Mina still slept, curled in her warm wrappings. As far as the professor could see, it was a natural sleep—if it was not, well, he could do no more for her than he had done already.

Having eaten, forcing down distasteful food, and taken a little brandy as a stimulant, Van Helsing picked up his bag—the one containing the special tools that he was going to need. Then, with a trembling inner anticipation, feelings he fought against acknowledging to himself, he began the steep climb to the castle's forbidding bulk.

He glanced back only once, before he had climbed very far. Mina would be all right while he was gone; she would simply have to be. He had no choice but to leave her here, unprotected, for a daylight hour or two. Van Helsing thought the worst thing that could happen to her would be an attack by wolves—real wolves, beasts of nature. But as to that she would have to take her chances. Though there might be danger to her body, yet her soul was safe! What he had to defend against was something terribly worse.

It was an hour later, and full daylight, when Van Helsing emerged from the gloomy castle gateway. He was staggering with fresh exhaustion, barely able to move. Cradled in his hands, against the newly blood-soaked fur of his outer coat, he was carrying the three vampire women's freshly severed heads. With hoarse cries the professor hurled the grisly objects, one by one, over the nearby precipice, so that they fell into the river far below.

As sunset drew near, Van Helsing, having slept and eaten again, was somewhat restored; and so, to his great relief, was Mina, who on awakening seemed almost normal. When she stared, as if puzzled, at the blood on his coat, he muttered a few words suggesting that it had come from the dead horses. She did not pursue the matter further.

Shortly after Mina had awakened, and the professor had cajoled her into drinking some hot tea, the two of them by mutual agreement moved from their overnight campsite to a nearby promontory from which they could better overlook the nearest road.

183

This was the way along which, if all their calculations as to routes and times were right, Dracula and his pursuers must approach.

Of course, if their calculations should be wrong . . . then the men Van Helsing was counting on might be already dead, and the vampire prince victorious after all.

Mina had been staring into the distance along the road for what seemed like hours. Now suddenly she announced: "He comes!"

Van Helsing squinted in the same direction, but was at first unable to discern any movement. When he took up a pair of field glasses, he was at last able to see something that made him cry out.

"They race the sunset—they may be too late—God help us!"

The howling of wolves rose from the dusky forest clothing the nearby hills and the mountains' lower slopes. In the distance, now readily visible with the glasses, a wagon and its mounted escort of Gypsies was racing closer at top speed. And—the professor's heart rose at the sight—four men on horses were in close pursuit of the wagon. A minute later Quincey Morris's unmistakable rebel yell was clearly audible on the crag where Mina and Van Helsing waited.

Puffs of smoke, followed by the faint crackle of rifle fire, announced that the Winchesters had been brought into action.

Some important idea had suddenly occurred to Mina; or perhaps she had heard a call, though her companion had heard nothing of the kind. For whatever reason, she had turned her back suddenly on the chase so plainly visible below and started to climb, with renewed energy, toward where the castle towered against a darkening sky.

The professor stared, then cried out: "Madam Mina! Wait!"

But she gave no sign that she had heard him. Van Helsing, worried anew, lumbered after her as best he could.

The wagon, following the road, traveled a longer course than the people who climbed on foot. Still, it was moving much faster than Mina and Van Helsing were able to negotiate the rough terrain between the loops of road. The vehicle went roaring and clattering past the man and woman as they climbed. Both could see it lurching on ahead of them, the driver whipping the exhausted horses, still escorted by a handful of Gypsies riding horseback.

And after them the hunters galloped.

The great leiter-wagon was almost at the castle when the four pursuing riders overtook it and did their best to force it to a halt. With gunfire, sabers, and huge knives, three Englishmen and an American fought their way through the fanatical defense put up by Dracula's remaining escort.

Harker leaped from his saddle onto the wagon, and its driver lashed at him with his whip; but Quincey Morris shot the man down.

The wagon, accompanied by its remaining escort and pursuers, all intermingled now, thundered through the tunnel and into the castle's courtyard.

Mina and Van Helsing, making the best speed afoot that they were able, followed. He could not manage to catch up with her, and lacked the breath to call to her.

Wolves were still howling all around them.

They stumbled into the courtyard only in time to see the conclusion of the fight.

Dr. Seward ran a Gypsy through with his saber, protecting Mina and Van Helsing.

Quincey, slashed in the back by another Gypsy, went down fighting.

Holmwood fired his pistol and finished off Quincey's assailant, the last of Dracula's allies.

Jonathan Harker, ignoring the fighting that still raged around him, concentrating with the intensity of a madman upon his own unshakable purpose, had just started to cut the ropes binding Dracula's box of earth to the wagon when the lid of the box exploded upward, and the pale-faced, white-haired figure inside burst out with a roar, grabbing for Harker's throat. Both men, struggling, fell to the ground.

Mina screamed in horror, as her husband, swinging his great, curved kukri knife, slashed his enemy's throat almost from ear to ear. Dracula's blood gushed out.

And at that moment Quincey, calling on his last reserves of strength, regained his feet and came forward in a diving lunge, to plunge his bowie knife into Dracula's heart.

The vampire's life was ebbing swiftly, yet he still had enough strength left to fling the Texan aside into the snow. Then Dracula, still proudly erect, eyes glaring as if into a distance only he could see, legs staggering, pouring gore from heart and throat, turned away from his enemies to begin a tottering retreat toward the door of the old chapel.

Mina moved quickly to grab up Quincey's Winchester. Then she rushed to take a stance between the dying monster and her victorious friends. To their vast astonishment, she leveled the rifle straight at her husband as he stood in their midst.

For the first time in hours—perhaps in days—Harker's murderous expression softened.

"Mina!"

Dracula, his face now horribly transformed, becoming a very countenance of death, turned to her also.

"Mina?" His tone was tender and loving.

For an agonizing moment she held the dying man's gaze. Then, when Dracula averted his face and resumed his dragging progress toward the chapel, Mina backed slowly after him. Still she held the Winchester resolutely leveled at the men.

Speaking into a taut silence, she demanded of the four still on their feet: "When my time comes, will you do the same to me? *Will you?*"

Holmwood would have rushed at her and tried to grab the weapon away, but Harker, understanding now, put out an arm to hold him back.

"No, let them go. Let her go."

Van Helsing nodded knowingly.

Mina backed slowly after Dracula into the dark doorway of the chapel. She never wavered in her determination to keep the men away from him, until what was about to happen could be concluded.

From inside, she pushed the massive door shut in their faces.

Outside, Van Helsing let the weapon he had picked up fall to the ground. Facing the chapel, swaying on his feet in weariness, he bowed his head, praying intensely.

Suddenly Harker cried out: "What is in there?"

Van Helsing looked up once. "It is the chapel."

No one asked him how he knew that, any more than they had asked him how all the dried blood came on his furs; but Harker accepted the answer as reassuring.

Once more the old man bowed his head and prayed: "Rest him . . . let him sleep in peace. We have all become God's madmen."

Meanwhile Dr. Seward was cradling the dying Quincey; there was nothing more that any physician or surgeon could do for him.

Inside the chapel, Mina and Dracula had both come to rest upon the very altar steps where, more than four centuries earlier, Elisabeth's dead body had lain.

She said now: "You cannot leave me. I want to be with you—always." And she gripped the handle of the bowie knife still protruding from his chest, and nerved herself for the effort to pull it out.

Dracula's own fingers, already wasted, as if by magic, to little more than bone, crept up the shaft to prevent her. His voice was only a rattling among dried bones and leaves.

He said: "You must let me die."

She stared down into his eyes; cradled him, kissed him, tenderly smoothed his white, matted hair. "No, please. I love you."

He shook his head, very slightly. "Mortal love can have no hold—on us. Our love will last for all eternity. Release me. Give me peace."

Outside the chapel door, Harker was pacing nervously. Arthur Holmwood, pacing, too, stopped suddenly to pound a futile fist against the wood.

Van Helsing held up a hand, indicating to both men that they should be still.

Inside the chapel, Mina had the perception that old altar candles, dead for centuries, seemed to be lighting themselves. Perhaps it was only that her tears dimmed her vision; or that the last glories of the sunset were coming in so redly through the glass, which was still intact, of the tall window just behind the plain altar with its towering cross.

The shadow of that cross fell down the steps upon the two still-living bodies lying there.

The woman raised her body into a crouch and murmured to her beloved: *"An arrow flew through my window—a message was fixed to it. And it was too much. I could bear no more."*

Slowly, weakly, Dracula opened his eyes, to see who was bending over him. He smiled . . . it was Elisabeth.

Again she whispered to him. "I could not bear the thought of life without my prince. But I see you are not among the dead. You live, my love."

And now her capable hands—they were Mina's hands, and Elisabeth's as well—once more clutched the knife whose point lay in his still-undying heart.

Quaking, praying for strength to do what she must do, she closed her eyes and fell on him, driving the long bowie blade in to the hilt.

When Mina opened her eyes again, the face of the man beneath her was deathly still. It was quite young, and peacefully, beautifully human.

Slowly Mina got to her feet and moved toward the closed door of the chapel. At that moment Jonathan, unable to wait longer, pushed the barrier open and rushed in to take his wife in his arms. And Mina knew, by the joy in her husband's face when he beheld her, that the snow was not more stainless than her own forehead. The scarlet curse of the vampire had passed away. The warrior prince was at peace.

AFTERWORD
by Francis Ford Coppola

I think the first Dracula film I ever saw was the John Carradine *House of Dracula*. I adored Carradine, with his gaunt face and how he would actually lift his cape and turn into a bat—he is my prototype Dracula. . . .

I had read the book when I was pretty young and loved it. Then as a teenager, I was the drama counselor at a camp in upstate New York, and had a bunk of eight- and nine-year-old boys. I would read aloud to them at night, and one summer we read *Dracula*. And when we got to that chilling moment—when Harker looks out the window and sees Dracula crawling across the face of the wall like a bug—even those little boys knew, this was going to be good! . . .

When I read Jim's script, I thought he had made a brilliant innovation by using that history of Prince Vlad to set the frame for the whole story. It was closer to Stoker's novel than anything done before. . . .

I noted, watching all the other Dracula films, how much they held back from what was written or implied, how they played havoc with the characters and their relationships. In our movie, the characters resemble Stoker's in their personalities and function, including many characters that are often cut out. And then the whole last section of the book—when Van Helsing is uncovering

189

Dracula's weaknesses, and the Vampire Killers pursue him back to his castle in Transylvania, and the whole thing climaxes in an enormous John Ford shootout—no one had ever portrayed that. . . .

Doing justice to the complex character of Dracula was one of our main goals. He's been portrayed as a monster or as a seducer, but knowing his biography made me think of him as a fallen angel, as Satan. The irony is that he was a champion of the church, this hero who singlehandedly stopped the Turks, and then he renounced God because his wife was a suicide and was denied holy burial. When great ones fall, they become the most powerful devils—Satan was once the highest angel.

Man's relationship with God is sacramental; it's expressed through the symbol of blood. So when Dracula rejects God, blood becomes the basis for all kinds of unholy sacraments in the story: baptism, marriage, and Mass. . . .

Blood is also the symbol of human passion, the source of all passion. I think that is the main subtext in our story. We've tried to depict feelings so strong they can survive across the centuries, like Dracula's love for Elizabeth. The idea that love can conquer death, or worse than death—that she can actually give back to the vampire his lost soul. . . .

Usually Dracula is just a reptilian creature in a horror film. I want people to understand the historical and literary traditions behind the story. To see that underneath this vampire myth is really fundamental human stuff that everyone feels and knows. . . . Even if people today don't feel a sacramental relationship with God, I think they can understand how many people renounce their blood ties to the creation—to the creative spirit, or whatever it is— and become like living dead. The vampire has lost his soul, and that can happen to anyone.